RETALIATION

The second book of THE PENALTY.

by Ethan Marek

RETALIATION

Dedicated to my childhood hockey coaches

Dad and Joel Munson

STREAKS

The summer sun strikes down on the fresh tar. A small wall of wind pushes the green leaves in the trees. The plants are finally lush after a crucial winter. A dark-tinted suburban pulls into a parking space in front of an ordinary strip mall, but the last set of doors on the left belongs to a training facility called The Pond. It's a hockey facility that uses a smaller sheet of ice so players can focus on individual skills and small teams can play little area games. Hockey in Minnesota is something else, but when it's summer, hockey just feels weird. There's something different to it when you walk into a hockey rink and it's humid and muggy outside like you live in the tropics. It's also refreshing and exciting to play hockey in the off-season. After being in the heat all day, it's nice to play in the cooler arenas. Then, after playing on the ice and breaking a sweat, going outside is a luxury. A peanut butter candy bar and a tropical-blue energy drink finish the day off with a splash.

Annie kicks one of her tennis shoes out the suburban's door with the laces dangling in the air. She ties her shoe in the classic bunny-ear knot. Since the rink's going to be chilly, she grabs her sweatshirt from the passenger seat. After she shuts the door and throws her sweatshirt on, she walks to the front doors of The Pond. Her sweatshirt strings sway side to side in the warm wind. Before crashing into the cold, she pauses on the sidewalk and finds her cell phone buzzing. She answers it.

"Make it quick, Daniel," she says.

"When am I going to see him, Annie?" Daniel says.

"We discussed this already."

"You can't keep him hostage for long."

"He's mine."

"Yes, but he's also mine. Shouldn't we let him free to see both of us?"

"I don't want him near you. Especially with what happened."

"You're paranoid, Annie. He's our son, and he's old enough to make his own decisions."

"Have you forgotten the past already?"

"No. I haven't. I will never forget what happened, and that's exactly why I'm trying to keep Clayton safe."

"How dare you. I am his mother. I'll be protecting him from now on. I'll make the right decisions for my child."

"Have you forgotten the past, Annie?"

Annie shuts her phone and stuffs it in a pocket. She tightens her jaw before walking through the front doors of The Pond.

Another pair of doors sends Annie into the cold as it clenches onto her bare skin. The zamboni resurfaced the ice. The water puddles on the ice while it's in a slow freeze. Three bleachers sit on the side of the rink where hockey parents bundle up. Each bleacher has three rows of seating They're pretty small bleachers that are hard as a stone and cold as Neptune.

Annie pulls out her thin mittens and slides them on. She rubs them together as she watches her breath fog up in front of her. A couple of hockey players from one of the teams wait outside of a locker room. Their jerseys are black with some sort of showcase logo on them. They chit chat with each other while one of them pushes their knees down with their hockey stick.

Behind the players in black, a door opens. A few players dressed in white exit the far locker room and waddle to the other team. They hug one of the guys in black. Annie looks for her son as he pops out from the far locker room, dressed in white, and leans against the door, holding it open while watching the other players talk. Some of his other teammates must be waiting in the locker room.

Two referees exit their mini locker room. They move between the bleachers to reach the rink's door, propping it open to hop on smooth ice. The team in black skates onto the ice first, then follows Clayton's team. Annie notices a cappuccino machine by the locker rooms. She walks over to it, grabs a few coins from her pocket and slides them into the machine. She selects a vanilla cappuccino. The machine shoots out a plastic cup. Hot cappuccino pours out of the spout and begins to fill the cup. Steam rises from the drink as it continues to pour. Once it finishes, a plastic door slides open so she can grab her hot drink.

Annie ambles her drink to the bleachers. She sits on the bleachers to the right of center ice, the side of Clayton's team. The cold air breezes by as the players finish skating their warmup laps. The referee blows his steel whistle in commence of the puck drop. Both goalies on each team settle themselves in their nets. The goalie in black hits the net with the blade of his stick. The goalie in white takes a swig of water before throwing his blocker back on. Three players on each side skate to the center of the ice and prepare for puck drop. With one more peep of the whistle, the ref drops the puck. They battle.

Clayton stands on the bench with his teammates. The guy next to him points at something on the ice, and they both smile.

Another lady walks onto the bleachers and over to Annie. She situates her blanket and sets her purse down. "Hey, Annie!" the lady says.

"Charlotte," she says. "How are you?"

"I'm doing great. How are you?"

"Good."

"I can't believe they've graduated high school already."

"Right. Isn't it crazy how fast time flies?"

"I know. They're all grown up, and before we know it, they're going to be graduating from college with their degrees."

"Don't even get me thinking about that. It's too early."

"Right. It's weird to think they've finished high school so fast." A ting of the crossbar catches Charlotte's attention.

"Where's Justin at?"

Annie watches Charlotte's son, Justin, enter the game from their team's bench. "He just hopped on the ice."

"Let's hope he'll score some goals."

The goalie in white skates back as a player in black takes a hard slap shot. The puck flies to the upper shelf of the net, but the goalie swipes it away with his glove.

"Nice job, Jacob!" Annie says.

"Woooo!" Charlotte yells.

"He's going to do great in college."

"I hope so. I've been so nervous for him this past year."

The referee blows his whistle and drops the puck. Annie watches Clayton win the faceoff. Clayton's team breaks it out of their defensive zone as the right-winger carries the puck near the offensive zone. The winger crosses over the blue line on a 2v2, his centerman rushing to the net.

A player in black rushes beside the centerman, keeping him covered. The winger sends a hard pass to his centerman, but the opponent shoves his stick down on his breezers. The centerman falls on the ice with the player in black falling behind him. The centerman slides headfirst into the boards as the opponent's body crashes into him. A loud crack echoes in the cold air.

Annie springs off the cold bench, cupping a gloved hand around her mouth. Her eyes stare wide as the refs push the players back to their benches. As they clear the area, one player lies on the ice frozen like an iceberg. She notices the number on the back of his jersey. 11.

Charlotte watches Annie whip her cup of cappuccino at the glass as she hurries to the rink's door. She runs onto the ice and kneels down by her motionless son. While Annie screams into the still air, Charlotte watches the cappuccino streak down the glass. It covers the glass in its stickiness as it drips all the way down to the empty cup. The steam rises in the air and stirs in the cold.

FRESH FIELDS

It's been some time since the air conditioner cranked on. Minnesota has finally met summer with a wall of humid air. The sun's beams strike right through my window, shimmering inside like invisible ripples on a lake. It comforts me to see the warm light again, especially after that dark winter. Not one cloud fluffs in the sky. A gentle breeze pushes the trees outside my window. The leaves wave at me while butterflies flutter their wings around the roses, and the birds tweet their songs upon the branches.

"Liam," Ash says. "Are you ready?"

"Yeah," says I. "I'm ready to dominate."

"I need to see the Wild beat Chicago at least once."

"Agreed."

"Those dang Blackhawks."

"I mean, it only makes sense that the State of Hockey should have the best NHL team in the country."

A popup message appears on the television. "Do you have a

charger?" Ash says.

"Ugh," says I. "Yes. I should anyhow."

"What do you mean?"

"I don't know where it is."

"Is it behind the TV?"

"I don't think so." I push the flat screen to the edge of my dresser. Nothing but dust sits on top. I push the television back and search my drawers. The top drawer holds my socks and underwear, and the next two drawers from under have my shorts and sweats, most of them coming from high school hockey. I wish I could keep getting clothes from the school, but I graduated. Ash and I are done playing high school hockey, our high school career is over. There's no turning back in time, and I know our lives shall continue, but I'm already starting to feel the pain of missing it all. I always tried to take the alumni's advice in high school to live every experience to the fullest, but even when I tried, it just never worked. Sometimes, I think I tried so hard to have a good time in high school that it didn't feel true to the heart, and I definitely stressed about my future dream of becoming a movie maker. But no one was really there for me, and I had to put in the work to get things done.

"Where do you think it could be?" Ash says.

"Oh," says I. "I know where it's at."

"Where?"

"The Barn."

"Why is it at the rink?"

"Well, Charlie brought his gaming console into the locker

room after its renovations."

"Didn't they have chargers though?"

"There's ended up tearing, and they asked me to game with them one night. So, I drove on over with my charger and we gamed all night."

"Welp, I guess the Blackhawks are just going to have to wait to be demolished."

"I guess so."

A knock at my bedroom door catches my attention. My mom opens the door and peers her head in. "How you boys doin?"

"We're doin good," says I. "We were gonna run to the rink to pick up my charger."

"Charger to what?"

"For my controller."

"Oh. I see. What's it doing there?"

"Ugh . . . One night, after a game, me, Jake, and Charlie gamed in the locker room and I brought the charger back from home."

"Wait. You were at the rink—"

"I went home to take a shower after our hockey game, and then they called me to join them."

"Oh. That makes sense."

"Yeah."

"Wait. Does this mean you guys gamed without me? You gamed without inviting your coach?"

"Maybe."

Mom laughs, and Ash chuckles with her. I grow a smile to

make my mother feel over-average with her comedy cap on.

"Well, I guess I'm going to have to eat those chocolate chip cookies myself then."

Ash catches my eyes and mouth prying wider and wider. He reflects like a mirror. Ash jumps out of his chair. We run down the hallway and down the stairs and into the kitchen. A pyramid of chocolate chip cookies sits on a plate in the dining room. We hustle over and sit in our pine chairs. We both take a fresh, warm cookie from the top and bite into it. It's lava to the tongue as it spits out chocolate sparks onto my taste buds. The chewiness sinks my teeth deep into a soft pillow. My mom brings us two tall glasses of milk and sets them on the table.

Ash gasps. "Thank you, Jenny," Ash says.

"You're welcome," she says.

While Ash chews on his second cookie, I scan out the window to my backyard forest. I spot a red cardinal flying from one tree and landing on another. The sound of pecking brings my focus to a woodpecker in one of the maple trees. It echoes through the other critters' sounds. I can't imagine leaving this place, especially for college. I'm actually not sure what I really want to do in my future. Filmmaking lingers in the back of my mind, but there's something else I want. I just can't put the puck in the net.

"Shall we go?" says I.

"Yes," Ash says.

"Okay, mom. We'll be back."

"Sounds good," she says. "Drive careful."

"I will."

Me and Ash head to my SUV. We hop inside the burning box while I try to start it as fast as possible. I twist the key in the ignition as the rubber seat burns my legs.

"Frick!" says I. A tingling sensation awakens in my feet.

"What?" Ash says.

I take my shoes and socks off. My burned, healing feet. They look like camouflage has been painted onto them with a bland color of purple and grey.

"What is it?" Ash says.

"Sorry. My feet were itching."

"I hate it when that happens."

"I know. Tell me about it."

I throw my socks and shoes back on, then I close my door and open the windows. After we throw our seatbelts on, I pull the car out of the driveway and head for The Barn. As we drive on the country roads, I find Ash looking out the window. As he watches the cornfields with their early sproutings, I glance at his hair which waves in the wind. I focus back on the road and stick a hand outside my window. The wind pushes my hand back as it swims in the wavy air. Ash sticks his hand out the window as well. He waves his whole arm out in the wind.

After a few more farm fields, we make it into our town of Kielstad and arrive at The Barn. We exit my car and walk to the front. There are some vehicles out front which can only mean there's a summer hockey camp going on for the Bantam players. Summer camp was fun in high school, but this summer, me and Ash are doing some sort of camp meant for alumni. I should talk

11

to my mom more about it because I believe we're leaving in a few days for it. Everything seems to be flying by so fast. We literally graduated like a week ago, and now we're going to be starting camp and staying there for most of the summer. Then before we know it, college will be flaring up in the fall. Man, what is life right now?

Ash leads our way through the double set of french doors. The front area has new rubber mats on the floor. Out the viewing windows are Bantam boys playing a game of street hockey on the concrete rink. The ice always melts in The Barn, so usually, we'd have dryland in here and travel to Prior Lake for some ice time. It's great to see some younger boys enjoying their time together. Even their coaches are playing with them.

We move down to the long hallway. The new rubber flooring runs all the way down to the end wall, way past the game doors. I can still smell the fresh paint that was put on the walls. The walls have the same design as last time. We pass by the dryland room and walk under all the caged lights till we hit our locker room. Ash pushes the door open as the lights flash on. My eyes sparkle in the bright white lights. Our locker room has doubled in size with the new renovations. Stalls outline every wall, and more stalls create an island in the middle of the room. The television hangs above the shower room which was built on the right when you walk in the door.

I spot my charger as it dangles from the gaming console, sitting on a plastic square platform that was screwed in under the flat screen. "There you are," says I. I unplug the cord from the console and turn around to find Ash staring at the stalls.

"Memories, huh," he says.

"Yeah. Brings them back, doesn't it."

"It does. It really does."

"You know, sometimes, I wonder . . . What would it be like if they were still here?"

I watch Ash prop open the cubby door to what used to be Chester's stall. Then I look at Finn's stall. They both sit empty in the silence. Small puddles build in my eyes. I lay a hand on Ash's shoulder. "Me too," he says.

FOREST FRIENDS

A green forest protrudes the hot summer sun from above. Two teenage boys mountain bike on a dirt path in the middle of the woods. Plants brush their leaves on their legs as they zip by. The wheels crunch the dirt and the chains clank while they shift gears. Dust flies out from the wheels and hovers into a floating cloud. The boys pant while they push the pedals faster and faster like they're trying to keep the electricity flow going on a stationary bike. The boy in front checks to see if his friend is keeping up, but when he looks back in front of him, his front tire crashes into a bulging tree root that humps out from the ground. His body flies down a steep hill. He hits the ground and barrel rolls his way down to the bottom. His friend jumps off of his bike at the top and runs down the hill.

"Barrett," he says. "Are you okay?"

Barrett surveys the area. "I think so." His friend reaches a hand and helps him stand. "Thanks, Louie."

"Looks like you got a few scrapes."

Barrett studies his arms, finding a huge scrape on his right and a smaller burn on the left. His kneecaps also seem to have been skinned with a cheese grater. "I'll just throw some mud on it I guess."

"You know what they say: hockey players are tough."

"Yes. We're strong. We're built to be pushed around." Louie turns around and squints in the distance. He searches through the plants and trees for something. "Louie, whatchu up to?"

"Shhhhhh," Louie says.

"What? What is it?" Barrett says.

"Is there a stream over here?"

Barrett walks in front of Louie and through the shrubbery. He turns around to find Louie just standing there, staring at him with confusion. "C'mon," Barrett says.

Louie sneaks in a small smile and follows Barrett through the thick shrubbery. While their legs itch from the surrounding plants, their feet crush weeds along the way. Mosquitos fly in and out from their ears, buzzing their wings in harmony. Barrett plants his hand on a tree, scanning it. Louie walks up to him and discovers the rushing stream. The water flows around rocks and makes little trickling waterfalls. The water is about ankle-deep and is clear as glass. Barrett takes his shoes and socks off and sets them next to the tree. He takes a foot and settles it into the water. His foot sinks into the mushy sand from under the flowing coolant. It feels like a cold glass of iced lemonade. Barrett steps his other foot in and saunters to the middle of the stream.

A huge rock bathes on the other side of the stream. Barrett smiles in excitement, then turns around to Louie who stands still by the tree. "What are you waiting for?" Barrett says.

Louie smiles. He throws his shoes and socks off to the side and leaps into the stream. Water droplets splash out from his jump and sprinkle on Barrett's body. Barrett grows a smile. He takes his hands and smacks the surface of the water, splashing Louie with sprinkles now. Louie smacks more water back at Barrett as they end up having a splash war. Their clothes dampen while soaking up all the water. Their shirts bag over, appearing as if they're like a men's extra-large.

They run over to a rock that pokes out in the middle of the flowing stream. A small waterfall flows beside the rock. Louie sits on it, swinging his feet in the waterfall, and Barrett rests on top. Barrett finds some mud on the side land and smears it on his scrapes and burns. While he reaches for some more mud, he finds a worm wiggling through. He gently picks it up with his fingers and evaluates it. It slithers around his fingers.

Louie watches his feet swish through the water. He cups his hands and reaches down as if it were a bucket in a wishing well. He brings the cup of water up to his face and drinks it. The water is crystal-clear, rushing down Louie's throat with its cool touch. He brings his face down to the stream and rubs the water on his face. It cleans all the sweat away. His hair turns into a mop as he tosses it all over his head.

A crack of thunder breaks in the sky. Barrett and Louie search through the outlying trees where a dark wall cloud storms into sight. "I guess it's time to go back," Barrett says.

"I think you're right, but I do love it out here," Louie says.

"It's awesome."

They hop off the rock and head for the tree. Rolling their socks up, they force their wet feet through the cotton. Once the shoes slide on, they head over to Barrett's bike. Barrett stares at his bike, lying on the ground in filthy muck.

"Uh oh," Louie says.

"Looks like we're gonna be walking."

Barrett walks his bike up the hill with the rusty chain dragging in the dirt. It's all tangled up in the gears. They reach the top of the hill as Louie lifts his bike from the ground. Raindrops splatter on their heads. They chuckle. Their feet begin to hustle on the dirt as they head down the trail.

They find their exit to Barrett's steep backyard. The rain picks up as the darker portions of the clouds move upon them. They run their bikes up the slippery slope. Some of the mud on Barrett's scrapes start to wash away. A flash of lightning startles them and kicks them into high speed to the top of the hill. They run onto Barrett's gravel driveway and into his garage. The rain downpours with another crack of thunder. It shakes the concrete beneath their feet.

"Wow," Barrett says. "We made it just in time."

"Honestly," Louie says.

From inside the garage, the house door opens. An older lady stands in the doorway, wiping her hands with a kitchen towel. She chuckles at the boys. "Man, you guys look like you've gone for a swim." She notices the scrapes on Barrett's knees. "Did you fall off your bike again?"

"Yeah."

"Here. Let me go get you some bandages."

"Thanks, Grandma."

She turns around and bumps into Barrett's mom in the kitchen. "Oh!" Grandma says. "You scared me."

His mom chuckles. "Sorry for that. I just turned the corners of the stairs and didn't even see you."

Grandma laughs. "I was gonna go get Barrett some bandages. He fell off of his bike again."

"Oh no. That's no fun."

Grandma leaves the kitchen and passes in between the two dining rooms. One of the dining rooms is on the left, which contains an old brick fireplace. The other dining room is on the right, after you pass the wall with the wall-phone that is. Barrett's parents never use that dining table; it's always cluttered with Grandma's and Grandpa's paperwork.

Next, she passes by the front door entrance, behind the wall of their cluttered dining-room office, and in the back-left corner of the main level is a sunken living room where two round carpeted steps lead into. That sunken room contains Grandma's and Grandpa's golden couch. Barrett always calls it the golden couch room.

The whole house is covered in a dirty, shaggy carpet, but it's truly cozy to the feet. It's almost like no one should have to put socks on to keep their feet warm inside. And finally, behind the front entrance is the master bedroom and bathroom. That's where Barrett's grandparents sleep. This is their house, and Barrett's family moved in with them.

Barrett's mom walks to the house door and checks his scars.

"Ouu," she says. "Owie."

"Nah," Barrett says. "It doesn't hurt too bad."

"Let me get you cleaned up here." She walks inside and rips off some paper towels from its holder and takes them into the garage. She wipes the mud off from his scrapes and burns that stuck to his skin in the downpour.

Grandma enters the garage with her first aid kit. She sets it down and kneels on the floor. She pulls out a few alcohol wipes and big, bulky bandages. "Here's a few wipes, Julie."

"Thank you," she says.

Julie wipes down Barrett's scrapes with the wipe. Louie can see him squeezing his eyes shut, fighting through the sharp stings. Grandma hands Julie the bandages. Julie does her motherly honor, sticking them on for Barrett. Grandma closes the first aid kit. She heads inside of the house.

"There," Julie says. "All better."

"Thanks, mom," Barrett says.

"You're welcome, sweetie. Let me go get you guys a towel so you can clean up." She leaves Barrett with a kiss on the forehead.

Barrett and Louie chill in the garage, watching the downpour.

SHOOTING STARS

The stars twinkle like fireflies in the dark. The cool summer breeze drifts by and wiggles the tips of the trees. Crickets cricket in the grass, and an owl whoos in my backyard forest. I inspect the trees for an owl, but it's too dark. I lay back and watch the stars with Ash from my roof. We've always enjoyed climbing out through the window at night and looking into the depths of space. Every friendship has its thing, and ours is watching the stars in the night sky.

"Are you ready for tomorrow?" Ash says.

"I don't know," says I. "I don't really know what to expect."

"Are you nervous?"

"I'm a little nervous with meeting new people."

"Nah, you'll be fine. There's nothing to worry about."

"What are we gonna be doing at camp anyways?"

"I don't really know."

"I mean, we stay there for like the whole summer."

"It didn't really say on our invitation, but I do know that it's a brand-new camp."

We focus back on the stars for a while. The owl still whoos somewhere in the back. A shooting star streaks across the sky in front of our eyes.

"Make a wish," Ash says.

I close my eyes to make my wish. Once my mind swirls around with its magical words, I pop back into reality, tilting my head on the shingles towards Ash. "You know, sometimes, I feel like Finn and Chester are with us," says I. "Do you ever feel that?"

"Sometimes. I like to think they're always with us. I mean, I'm not really religious but I still like to think they are."

"I think I feel their presence from time to time. It sometimes freaks me out because there'll be this feeling when I'm asleep."

"Really? What does it feel like?"

"It feels like I turn into a cub, you know? It's like they make me feel comforted." We look back to the twinkling stars. Another cool breeze swifts by.

"They would've loved this," Ash says.

"Yeah," says I. "They really would've loved this."

"What did you wish from that star?"

"It's a secret."

"What? C'mon. Tell me."

"But then the wish won't come true. I have to keep it a secret."

"Can I tell you mine?"

"Of course, if you want to that is."

"I wished for our futures to be successful. I want us to succeed and achieve our dreams. I want you to become the movie maker you've been destined to be, and I want to save lives in the Army. It's just that I stress about it all, and sometimes I'll look down on myself."

As sweet as that chocolate may be, it tasted bitter to me. Still not sure what my future holds with college. "I'm with ya on that. We all stress our futures out while we should be living in the present. But yet, even when I tell myself that, I end up doing it anyway."

"Why?"

"Why what?"

"Why do you keep on stressing?"

I find the North Star in the twinkling twilight, one of the brightest stars in our sky. "I stress because I love it. I don't know what I would do in life without it. Without stress, I don't think I'd be fighting for what I believe in. I don't think I'd be fighting for what I love most."

Ash turns his head to me again. "You're going to make some awesome fricken movies in your future." I grow a large smile. "I'm lucky to have a friend like you."

"I'm happy we're friends," says I. "I wouldn't change it for anything."

"Should we get to bed for the bus tomorrow?"

I pivot to him. "Maybe just a few more minutes."

We smile and gaze back into the thriving night sky.

THE DANGLE

The morning grass drinks the remaining puddles. Early birds tweet
as the sun rises over the trees. Barrett wakes in his bed from the
rising light. He gives his arms and legs a nice stretch, releases a
yawn, and looks out the window. Below him, Louie sleeps on the
floor with a small blanket and pillow, lying right beside Barrett's
bed. Barrett throws his blanket off and crawls to the end of his
bed. He keeps quiet while he walks over to his closet and grabs a
t-shirt. He moves over to his drawers on the far wall and digs for
shorts, underwear, and socks. When he turns around, he finds
Louie's luggage under the windows.

Louie opens his eyes. He blinks with the morning light
shining through the windows, rubs his eyes out, and lifts his chest
off the ground.

"Good morning," Barrett says.

"Mornin," Louie says.

"Ready for the big day?"

"Yeah, I think so." Louie notices his clothes on the floor. "Did you pack yet?"

"I probably should, shouldn't I?"

"Yeah. What time is it anyway?" Louie reaches for his charged cell phone by his head. He checks the time. "Dang, we leave in three hours."

"When's the bus leave?"

"Noon."

"I wish time would move faster. I don't want to spend another minute here."

"Why's that? Don't you like home?"

"This isn't home. This is my grandparent's place my parents are renting out."

"Well, I know that. You lost your home in that financial crisis." Barrett throws a clean pair of underwear aside and throws on his shorts. "What aren't you telling me, Barrett?"

"It's nothing really."

"Just tell me, dude. It helps to speak it out."

"I'll tell ya on the bus. Sound good?"

"Of course. Whatever makes ya feel better."

Barrett's stomach grumbles. "Well, are ya hungry?"

"I'm not super hungry, but I think we should probably eat before the ride. It's going to be like a four-hour bus ride."

"Where's the camp again?"

"Somewhere in a forest. I think it's south of the Boundary Waters."

"Imma bring headphones if that's the case. You should too."

Louie pats his pockets. "Got em."

"Sweet. Let's go downstairs and see what we have to eat."

Louie untucks himself from his blanket. He throws his clothes on, folds the blanket up, and enters the hallway with Barrett. They walk down the L-shaped stairs, passing a hexagon-shaped window and cuckoo clock on their way to the dining room. To the left of the dining room is a sliding door that leads out to the screened-in porch. The sunlight shines through the trees and shimmers inside the home.

Passing the brick fireplace and wall phone, Barrett and Louie make their way to the kitchen. Julie's standing by their cupboard full of cups and plates. Grandma and Grandpa keep their left side of the kitchen, and Barrett's family gets the right side. The left side contains the grandparents' fridge, and there's a serving hatch in the wall which views into their dusty dining office. Barrett's family has the oven and dishwasher on their side which everyone gets to use. A farm sink divides the kitchen by the back wall, looking out to the front yard and gravel driveway. In the middle of the kitchen is a spacious island with a stovetop on it.

Barrett finds his mom examining the inside of a glass. She pulls out hair and a clump of dust from inside.

"Hey, mom," Barrett says.

Julie jumps around to find Barrett and Louie. "Hey."

Barrett looks to Louie. "Let's see what we have in the cupboards."

Julie sets the glass in the sink. While Barrett and Louie are attracted to the shelves of food, Julie moves to a tall cupboard

25

door which contains the trash can. She throws the filthy clump of hair away and heads downstairs.

Barrett rummages through the canned goods and baking supplies. Other snacks laze on the shelves, but nothing attracts him for breakfast. "I think I know what we could have," Barrett says.

"Do you now?" Louie says.

"Are you good with pizza for breakfast?"

"Heck yeah, dude."

"Sweet. Let me run downstairs quick."

Louie sits on top of the counter and pulls his phone out. Barrett strolls to the open basement door which is in the kitchen. He walks down another L-shaped stairway and makes it to the basement. Barrett's living room sits in the basement next to the brick fireplace. The furnace room, bathroom, and storage room are on the far-right wall. His parent's bedroom is right across the living room. The basement sinks deeper in the back, and it gets darker the further in you look. A pool table and broken ping pong table stand in the dark.

Barrett hears his mom complaining about something to Jim, his father. Their bedroom door is peeked open. He continues around the fireplace, taking a right to find three of the storage doors. The one on his left is where Barrett's storage and fridge are located. The other two rooms contain Grandma's creepy dolls and their deep freezer. There are many more boxes in those rooms, but most of them are covered in dust and cobwebs.

He turns left into the storage room and finds the freezer. He opens the door and grabs his pizza. Once he closes the door and turns around, he stops dead in his path. His mom's spider decoration for Halloween lies in the middle of the doorway. It's a huge black, fuzzy spider with glowing red eyes, but he swears the decoration had longer legs. He focuses on it, then notices it's not a Halloween decoration. That spider wasn't there when he walked in, and he didn't hear anything fall. He squeezes onto the pizza and takes deep breaths. He squeezes his eyes shut while taking in one last breath. Barrett opens his eyes and bolts. He hurtles the fuzzy spider and catches himself on the other storage room door. He looks back and sees the spider crawling under the door. Barrett recognizes the creepy crawler as a wolf spider, but he's never seen one so gigantic in his life. It's the size of his hand with its legs spread out.

Barrett passes the fireplace, his mother still complaining about something, but this time she sounds like she's weeping. He heads up the stairs while skipping every other step. He makes it to the top and cranks the oven on. The oven is so dated; it sits in between the taller cupboards like you'd see in the eighties. The numbers on the dial also broke in the past, but it still works. Barrett removes the wrapping on the pizza and slides it in.

"Alright," Barrett says. "It should be ready in like fifteen."

Grandma enters the kitchen on the other side of the island. "Barrett," she says.

"Oh. Hey, Grandma."

"Did you track in mud last night?"

"No? Me and Louie got all cleaned up outside."

"Well, that's strange. There's mud all over the carpet leading over to the stairs."

Barrett discovers a small dirt path from the house door. "Me and Louie double-checked our feet though. We didn't want to track any of it in."

"Well, all I know is that there's mud on my carpet and you're the only one who could've done this."

"I swear, Grandma. That wasn't us."

"Well whoever it was, you boys are cleaning that up before you leave."

Barrett hears a stomping rampage coming from the basement stairs. Louie gazes from his cellphone and over to the basement door. Julie comes to the top of the stairs and stops. "What's going on?"

"I was just having a conversation with your son."

"And what about?"

"Well, if you look at the carpet, you can see they tracked in mud last night."

Julie glares at Barrett and Louie. "Did you boys track in mud last night?"

"No. We checked our feet before walking in. We even double-checked."

Julie faces Grandma. "I don't want you speaking to my son."

"Excuse me?"

"You heard me. You're done speaking with him."

"I'm his grandmother—"

"STEP grandmother."

"And I don't have to listen to you. This is my house."

"This isn't your house. This is Grandpa's house." Grandma chuckles. Jim walks up behind Julie. Julie continues her conversation. "What's so funny? He's the one paying the bills while you're here shopping online for clothes."

Grandma moves from the kitchen island and in front of my mom. "I'll push you down these stairs."

Julie points at Grandma's face and smiles. "That's a threat. I'm gonna call the police."

"Hold on, sweetie," Jim says.

"No, Jim. I'm calling the cops." Julie heads down the steps as Jim talks with Grandma. She begins to tell him the story of Barrett and Louie tracking in mud. Louie jounces to his phone. Barrett stands by the oven and looks down at his hands. They both shake, and he tries to stop them, but he can't. He can feel his sores drying out, and his eyes blur with water as they fill up into dams. He holds in the tears the best he can.

Grandma leaves the room and heads back into her bedroom. Grandpa must be at work right now. Jim looks over to Barrett and rolls his eyes, then walks downstairs to the basement. Barrett turns around and sees Louie's eyes frozen on his phone. "Sorry you had to see that, Louie. I don't know what just happened."

"It's alright, dude."

Barrett leans over the kitchen sink and finds his mother walking down the gravel driveway to the cal-de-sac. She stands behind the pine tree out front near the mailboxes.

Barrett opens the oven door. The pizza's crust is at a light brown. The cheese can probably use more time, but Barrett pulls it out anyway. He digs through a drawer and pulls out the pizza cutter. He cuts it into eight triangles and takes Louie to the dining table. They take a slice from the cardboard and dig into the hot, cheesy pizza.

While they eat in the dining room, Barrett can see two cop cars pull up to mom in the cal-de-sac. The cops run to her, one of them handing her a few tissues. She wipes her eyes, and he assumes she begins to tell the story of what happened. Barrett takes small bites out of his pizza, chewing it like a sloth.

"I'll be right back," Barrett says. He puts the half-eaten pizza down on the cardboard and runs upstairs. He turns right at the top to the blue bathroom; the tub is blue, the toilet is blue, the walls are blue, and the sink's blue. He closes the door and locks it. He bends over the sink and rests his hands on the counter. He assesses himself in the mirror. Barrett wants to release his tears into a lake, but he can't find himself able to do so. It's almost as if it's winter again and the lakes just froze over.

He exits the bathroom and walks downstairs. When he makes it back to the dining room, he can hear the cops talking with Grandma in the golden couch room. He can't see them with a wall dividing them, but he can hear her talking about him. Barrett continues on his pizza as Louie is on his third. The cops begin to move into the dining room with Grandma following behind. She finds Barrett and Louie sitting there eating pizza.

"Are you serious?" Grandma says.

"What?" says one of the cops.

"They were sitting here the whole time when I was speaking

with you. They overheard me speaking my part to you guys."

"And what do you want us to do about it?" says the cop.

"Well, arrest them."

The cops sneak a smile at each other. Grandma turns around and storms into her bedroom. The cops say their farewells to Barrett and Louie, then exit out the house door. The cops stroll with Jim down the gravel driveway and meet Julie in the cal-de-sac. They speak out front for a while as Barrett and Louie finish their pizza. The cops head into their cars and leave.

Julie and Jim return to the house. They go downstairs. "I should probably start packing," Barrett says.

"I'll come help ya," Louie says.

Barrett leaves the crumby cardboard on the table as they walk past the cuckoo clock and up the L-shaped stairs. Barrett closes his bedroom door behind Louie. He pulls out two empty luggage bags from the closet and throws out a pile of shirts and sweatshirts. He moves over to his drawers and tosses out underwear, socks, shorts, and sweatpants onto the floor. Louie and Barrett fold the clothes and pack them.

"Don't forget to grab your bathroom supplies too like your toothbrush and towel," Louie says.

"Thanks, Louie."

"And don't forget your charger."

"Nah. That's definitely something I won't forget."

Barrett finds the door opening up from behind him. His mom interrupts with still tears. "Barrett," she says. "Pack up your favorite things."

"I am packing. Our bus leaves in a couple of hours."

"No. I'm sorry, sweetie, but you can't go anymore."

"What?"

"We're moving out. Dad and I will get us a hotel room today. We don't know how long we're gonna stay there but we hope to find a place soon." She turns around and begins to head out.

"No, mom." She turns around and stares into Barrett's watering eyes. "I'm leaving with Louie. I'm going on that bus."

"Barrett," she says. "Pack up your things—"

"No! I'm done living in this miserable life, mom. I'm done suffering every fricken day of my life while watching you and dad depressed because of your money problems. I just want to be happy and have fun with my friends. I'm sorry, but I'm leaving."

She plays with her fingernails. She turns and walks away, shutting the bedroom door behind her. Barrett's lips tremble as his hands shake again. He looks outside to the daylight and hears the birds tweeting their melodies. He watches his Grandma's car zip-out, kicking the dust into clouds. He drops his first set of tears as they streak down his cheeks.

Louie continues packing his clothes for him. Barrett observes his mom in front of the garage, dropping his hockey bag, and two of his hockey sticks, on the ground. Barrett whimpers. He squeezes his eyes shut and lets the lake fill up beneath him.

Louie stops folding his clothes and stands next to him. He places a hand on his shoulder as Barrett hides his face within his arms. Louie bear hugs Barrett as the sun rises over the trees.

THE GREAT GRIFFIN

Me and Ash wait outside of The Barn with my mom. The bus is picking us and some of the other kids up from here as it's a good midpoint for everyone. I pull my bag out from the trunk with my sticks and rest them upon the black tar. Ash also takes his bag and sticks from mom's trunk. My mom grabs our luggage and stands them up on their feet. She searches the trunk and digs through the seats for any forgotten items.

"Do you guys have everything?" she says.

"I believe so," says I. "I'll just check my bag one more time."

"Yeah," Ash says. "I always feel like I'm forgetting something."

I zip my bag open to find the stench of old hockey sweat swarming my nose. The last time I wore my gear was in high school, but the stench stays with you forever. I dig through my equipment. I check to see that I have my compressions, my knee pads, socks, breezers, chest pads, elbow pads, and helmet. I've also snuck my beanie hat into my bag without my mother questioning about the summer heat. I dig to the sides and find my brand-new skates at the bottom. There's something inside one of them. I stare at it.

"All good here," Ash says.

"Same here," says I. "I got everything."

"Well," mom says. She squeezes me in a bear hug. Her chin settles on my shoulder blade. We begin to sway side to side for a little bit as she streams down tears. "I'm going to miss you guys." She walks over to Ash and gives him a bear hug too. "Let me help you guys with your luggage."

We grab our hockey gear and head to the coach bus. A younger man wearing a Twins baseball cap opens the few remaining storage areas under the bus. The door pops open and rises up in front of the window seats. He turns around to find us walking forth to him with our gear. He takes his baseball cap off.

"Howdy, folks," he says.

"Hi," says I.

"Welcome to the Great Griffin!" He looks at my mom who stands behind us with our luggage. "Pardon me. I forgot to introduce myself." He confronts my mom with an open hand. My mom takes it in hers and shakes. "My name is Steve." He steps back to look at me and Ash. "I'm your guys' bus driver."

"Nice to meet you," Ash says. He rolls his eyes at me. Ash heads behind Steve and sets his hockey bag under the bus. I join him and set my bag next to his. We lay our hockey sticks right next to our bags.

Steve juts in front of my mom again. "Well, let me help ya with that."

"Thank you," mom says. "That's very kind of you."

"Anything to help you, ma'am. Your kids are going to have a blast. I'm going to deliver them in one piece and make sure they enjoy their journey."

My mom points to me. "Actually, that's my son. I brought Ash along because they wanted to arrive together."

Steve laughs. "Well isn't that funny." He takes our luggage and sets them next to our hockey bags. "There ya go, boys. You're all boarded up."

I walk to my mom while she holds her arms open one more time. This time, her tears drip onto my shirt. "I'm going to miss you," she says. "What am I going to do without you?" She tightens her arms around me, then gives me a kiss goodbye. We break.

Me and Ash head to the front of the bus. The door to the bus is on the other side. I turn around and give my mom one last wave goodbye. She waves back while patting her tears with crumpled-up tissues.

Steve confronts my mom again for the third time. "I'll make sure they stay in good health." He turns around and makes his way to the front of the bus.

"Steve," mom says. "Wait." She scuttles to him. "Can I have your number? You know, just in case the boys' phones aren't working or something."

"Of course. It would be my pleasure."

The open bus door invites me and Ash into the bus. Ash hops

up the steps as I follow behind him. The stairs curve up to the left like a royal staircase. When we make it to the top, I stop dead in my tracks. Ash's eyes glisten in the blue ceiling which shines and shimmers like water. The leather seats align the walls of the entire bus. A flat-screen presents an animation of a mythical dragon-looking-creature with the bus name on the back wall:

THE GREAT GRIFFIN

The white marble floors reflect the blue lights from above. Ash strolls all the way to the back.

"C'mon, Liam," he says. "The back is ours."

Out of the right-side window, mom exchanges phone numbers with Steve. Ash looks at me, then gives me the impression that he's waiting. "Sorry. I'm coming." Ash sits at the end wall on the right. I plop next to him. "I guess we could've brought our backpacks on."

"They're fine in the luggage for now," Ash says, "or else we'd have things in the way."

"True."

"Crap."

"What?"

"I left my headphones in my bag."

"That's okay. I won't use my earbuds. I guess we'll have to talk with some other people."

I twist my body to glance out the window. Steve heads to the front of the bus, and my mom treks backward. I wave to her again.

She waves back and sends me a flying kiss. She turns around and finishes her tears in the car. I watch her drive out of the parking lot and disappear on the 30mph road.

"Aren't your parents gonna miss you?" says I.

"Yeah," Ash says. "Mostly my mom, but my dad will too at some point."

The crunching of rocks catches our attention. A suburban pulls up next to the bus. Two boys head out of the truck with one of their fathers. Steve meets with the dad. The boys begin to pack their stuff under the bus. The bus shakes a little as they toss the luggage on.

"Thanks for the ride, dad," Barrett says.

"You boys have fun. Work hard."

Barrett stops. "Wait, Louie." He turns around and runs to his dad. He wraps his arms around him. His father squeezes him in his hold. "I feel bad."

"Mom will be fine."

"She probably wanted to see me leave."

"Don't worry about her. She just has a lot going on right now." Jim kisses Barrett on his forehead. "Go on now." Barrett smiles at his father, then he turns around and runs with Louie to the bus doors. Barrett and Louie scurry up the curvy stairs as their eyes shimmer in shock.

"Dang, Louie," Barrett says.

"I've never seen a coach bus like this before," Louie says.

"Dude."

"What?"

"There's a fricken flat screen in the back."

Louie's face shines in the lights. "And the ceiling is literally lit, bro."

"It looks like water."

"Right."

I watch the two boys find their seats on the other side of the bus, sitting further among the bench. I meet eye contact with them. I smile, and then I look down at the floor. My heart begins to race, and I bounce my feet up and down off the marble floor.

"Nervous?" Ash says.

"No," says I.

"I think your leg says otherwise."

"Okay, maybe a little."

"You'll be fine. Talk to those guys."

"I don't know what to say."

"Say hi to them and ask what their names are."

"That's kinda awkward though."

"Ugh. Fine, let me start it off for ya." Ash lifts from his seat.

"Ash. No."

Ash walks up to them. "Hey, guys. My name's Ash, and over there's my soft cub, Liam."

"Hey," Barrett says. "I'm Barrett."

"And I'm Louie," Louie says.

"Nice to meet ya guys," Ash says. "So where are you guys from?"

"We're about fifteen minutes out from Kielstad," Barrett says. "Over in Prior Lake."

"Cool," Ash says. "You guys just graduated too, right?"

"Yep."

"Finally got out of that prison," Louie says.

"Tell me about it," Ash says. "I hated school. The only fun thing about it was hockey."

"You got that right," Louie agrees.

"The schools these days are just so strict. They wouldn't even let us have a senior prank."

"Same here, dude." Ash sits next to Louie.

Barrett looks at me. I pick at my fingernails. I bite them so often that I can't even pick at the nails. From the side of my eye, I catch Barrett strolling over to me. "What position do you play, Liam?"

"I'm a left-winger," says I.

"Oh, nice. Maybe we can be on a line together."

"You're a centerman?"

"No, actually. I'm a right-winger."

"Oh. I guess that would make sense." A small white sheet slips from my pocket and falls onto the marble floor.

"I think ya dropped something," Barrett says. He picks it up and turns it over. It's a photograph of me and Chester in our hockey gear. "This one of your lineys?"

"Um," says I. "Yeah. That was one of my lineys in high school."

"Is he coming on the trip?"

The marble floor distracts my eyes. "He's not here anymore."

"He moved?"

"No. He, um, passed away last season."

"Dude. I'm so sorry. Oh my God. Do you mind me asking what happened?"

"It's a long story."

"Sorry, man. If you need someone to talk to, I'm here for you."

"Thanks, Barrett."

The other crowd of boys arrives in the parking lot. They all hug their parents goodbye and throw their things under the bus. Ash comes back over and sits next to me. Barrett moves back by Louie. The other players walk in smaller pods ranging from two to five guys. They find seats to chill next to each other. Three guys sit across from me and Ash. Another player sits on the other side of Ash, alone. Everyone else fills the open seats upfront. Steve the bus driver hops up the steps and pulls out a clipboard from the front.

"Welcome to the Great Griffin, everybody!" Steve says. "My name is Steve and I will be your legendary bus driver. I will be your main export throughout your exciting journey. Whether you guys will be playing at a hockey arena or the camp needs groceries to feed, I am here to serve my duty as Steve: the legendary bus driver." He sets his hands on his waist and smiles at the water ceiling. "Now, before I forget, you guys need to check off your names so I can see that you're all here." He hands a clipboard and pen to the boys out front. We pass it around the bus and check our names off. Steve receives his clipboard back. "Awesome. It looks like we're all here."

Steve turns around and twists the key in the ignition. The engine kicks on. The sound of thunder rumbles the cabin as flashes of lightning strike inside of the water ceiling. Dark steel doors slam shut in front of our windows. The griffin on the back screen throws its wings up and begins flapping them, flying in circles through the air. It appears to get smaller as it gets further away, but then, it turns around and swoops across the screen. It flies from the flat-screen and onto the storm ceiling while the lightning flashes around its body, casting its silhouette in the darkness. It makes one final loop in the stormy clouds and freezes in front of the bus. The griffin gets into the same pose as it was on the flat-screen and stays on the ceiling.

Steve buckles up. He flips a few latches on his dashboard. The lights dim dark, and the front windshield blocks out the sunlight with some sort of shading technology. "All aboard the Great Griffin. Next stop, Camp Kelmo."

CAMP KELMO

The bus transitions from the smooth road and onto some sort of bumpy terrain. The steel cages blocked our view outside this entire bus ride. Me and Ash chit chatted along the way. I didn't really talk to anyone new, and no one really wanted to talk with me. Ash talked to the few guys across from us, but I didn't say a word. He does most of the talking for us. The other boys on the bus didn't seem to meet with each other. It's almost like we're in high school again; the clicky groups keep on thriving.

"Hang on, boys," Steve says. "It's going to get real bumpy here."

Ash gives me an excited smile. The back of the bus bounces us off our seats as it seems to roll down a hill. I try to look through the front window, but its shading technology blocks out the view. The griffin is still frozen on the stormy ceiling, and the flat screen on the back still reads THE GREAT GRIFFIN. I begin to slide to some other guys on my left as the bus sinks deeper into the hill. I grab onto the seat, and Ash does the exact same. One of the boys on the other side nudges into Louie as we all want to slide towards the front.

Soon enough, one of the guys in the back gets an idea. "Guys," he says. "Watch this." The boy moves onto the marble floor by Ash's feet. Another bump of the bus going down the steep hill sends the boy down the marble floor. He slides along the slippery slope while the boys cheer him on. He slides faster and faster down the floor, getting closer and closer to the front. The bus flattens out at the bottom of the hill as we all bounce in our seats again. The boy slows before his feet reach the curvy stairs. We applaud the boy as he stands back up and walks to his seat. He gives his ceremonial wave as he passes.

"Boys," Steve says. "Welcome to Camp Kelmo."

The steel doors clank as they pull up from the windows like a projector screen. Me and Ash turn around to find the view of the woods. A huge hill stands over us with green shrubbery and oak trees and pine trees. The dying sunlight fades over the hill. Over by Barrett and Louie, I see a small, round lake reflecting the darkening sky.

Ash taps me on the shoulder. "Liam, look over here." I twist my head out of my window again. A log cabin with screened-in windows and a wooden staircase sits along the grassy path. More cabins follow behind. Once the bus passes the living quarters, we roll in front of a building with a wooden sign above the door: Training Office. The bus turns to the right, then I see another building, much bigger with gigantic windows. Once the bus stops in place and parks, I turn around to find the griffin moving. It spins and flies to the back of the bus. Behind the griffin, the storm clouds sweep away and fade to the blue water again. The griffin transports from the ceiling to the flat screen and freezes in its standing pose.

"Alright, boys," Steve says. He stands in the front of the curvy stairs. "Stay settled in your seats. It's time to meet your Counselor." Steve walks down the curvy stairs and exits.

"Dude," Ash says. "This is sick."

"I'm so excited," says I.

"If we get bunks, we're sharing."

"I think the real question is, who gets bottom bunk?"

"Dibs."

"Sure. I can take top."

"Sweet."

Outside the other windows, over by the round lake, a few dirt patches in the grass are surrounded by wooden benches. Must be the area for campfires. On the right, closer to the cabins, a dock house sits on the shoreline of the lake. Canoes are neatly tied together with wooden paddles sticking out from them.

Footsteps walk upon the curvy steps. A man stops in front of the aisle. He's six-foot and has a bushy beard of a lumberjack. He wears casual shorts with a black overcoat on, hanging down near his feet. There's a white star embroidered on the sleeve of the coat, buttons line down the middle of it, and the collar is made up of dark animal fur. It looks like one of those overcoats you'd see a military commander wearing.

"Welcome to Camp Kelmo," he says. "I'm Counselor Campbell. I'm the guy who will be giving you the tour of the camp, as well as rules, protocols, curfew, and much more needed information you must know. You guys must stay with me at all times during this tour. I will help assign cabins for you guys later on in the tour, and then we'll all introduce ourselves around the campfires." Counselor Campbell stares at the boys on the left, then he stares at us on the right. "Let's get started."

We follow Counselor Campbell off the bus. Steve waits outside at the bottom of the stairs. He wishes us all fun on our journey as we hop off. We all group up in front of the campfires where Counselor Campbell stands on one of the wooden benches.

"Right here, near the shoreline of the lake, is our campfire area. We have four campfires set up with these nice wooden benches surrounding them. This is where we will meet tonight after assigning cabins." He jumps off the bench (not that it even mattered to go up there with his height) and leads us over to the Training Office. "Speaking of assigning cabins, this is mine. This is the Training Office. My headquarters are here, and it's always open before curfew. I'll be assigning you guys your cabins in there." He takes us over to the gigantic window building on the right. "Over here, we have the Cafeteria Cabin. This is where you boys will have brunch and dinner. Most of the day, you boys will be busy in your trainings." He points to something over our heads and near his office. "You guys probably saw the cabins on your way in. Those will be your living quarters. And across from your cabins is the dock. In your free time, you can swim, fish, or canoe.

Just let me know and I can get you set up." He looks back at the moon rising above the green trees. "Alright. I think it's time we assign cabins. You boys will have to assign six to a cabin as we have a total of thirty. So, pair up with some new people, grab your luggage, and meet me at my headquarters." Counselor Campbell leaves us in our grouping. The clicky friends glue together again. Me and Ash find Barrett and Louie walking over to us.

"You guys want to share a cabin?" Louie says.

"Yeah," Ash says. "That would be awesome."

"Who are the other two gonna be?" says I.

"We gotta find them," Louie says.

Two groups of six head to the office already. Eighteen guys left. We look around for any guys standing around. I notice two guys talking to each other while behind some other guys' backs. I walk over to them. One of the guys wears his hockey cap backwards, and the other has the hair of a shaggy bush. "Hey, guys. We got four in our group right now. Do you wanna join?"

"We got a group of six already," says the guy with the shaggy hair.

"Oh okay." I turn around and wander over to Ash again. I can feel the boys watching me walk away, and I can hear one of them chuckle. When I make it back to my group with Ash, I turn around to look back at them. They're already walking to the bus for their things.

There are twelve more guys left, including us four. Besides my group, there's another group of four. Two guys stand next to each other, looking around for a group. The other two seem to be friends, joining up with the other group of four. They shake hands with one another.

"Let's go ask those guys," Barrett says.

"Yeah," Ash says. "Let's do it."

Ash leads the way as the rest of us follow. The boy on the left has dark shaggy hair, and the one on the right splatters with freckles on his face.

"Hey," Ash says. "You two wanna join our group?"

"Looks like we have to," says the shaggy boy.

"Sweet. Let's go get our stuff and get in line."

We head on over to the bus, throw our hockey bags and sticks next to the other ones in the grass, then we grab our luggage and carry them with us to the long line in front of the Training Office. Looks like we fall in last behind all the other groups.

It's not the first time I've been last in line.

While the moon rises higher over the lake and the sun's light fades out from the sky, we finally make it to Counselor Campbell. We all walk inside and stand in front of his desk. A room sits off to the right and left. On the right, a doorway flows into a sitting area. On the left, the door is shut. It probably holds his bedroom since he said this was his cabin.

"Looks like you guys are my last group," Counselor Campbell says. "Alright. Give me your names one-by-one, then I'll send you to your cabin."

Ash takes lead. I follow after Ash and write my name on the blank line. Barrett and Louie sign their names, and the other two boys finish the sheet off. I guess we forgot to ask them what their names were.

Counselor Campbell looks over the sheet. "Okay, boys. A few standard ground rules before I send you off. Curfew is at 10 pm. All of you must be in your cabins by then. No wandering outside will be necessary. There are Hunters surrounding the camp, protecting us from wild coyotes and bears that roam around at night. You wouldn't want to be mistaken by one of them as an animal. Once the morning sun rises, you are free to stick around your cabins outside. If you want to take a canoe or grab fishing poles, you must come here and contact me. You have a restroom in the cabin, so you won't need to walk out to find one. Any questions?" We shake our heads no. "Alright, then." He hands over a key with a hockey lace looped around the keyhole to Ash. "You guys will be down in the farthest cabin: Cabin #5. The campfire meet-n-greet will start at nine sharp."

We exit the Training Office and walk down the grassy path our bus drove on. We pass under the huge oak trees that tower along the shoreline, the other cabins, and the dock house with the canoes, ending up at our cabin: Cabin #5. Ash leads the way up the steps and to the patio area. Four custom wood chairs sit on the patio. Ash twists the hockey lace key in the lock and opens the screened-in door.

He flicks on the light switch. One bunk bed lies to the right, the two other bunks are on the left. The bathroom is in the back-right corner. There are screened-in windows on each side of the front door. Ash picks front bunk on the left side, which sits back to back with the other one across from the bathroom. He settles his luggage down on the floor and crashes on his bottom bunk. I climb up the wooden supports to my upper bunk. My bed has a pillow with a tan cover and blanket. The blanket is actually nice like the lighter ones in hotels.

Barrett and Louie take the bunk that's back to back with us. The other two boys take the outlier bunk right in front of the bathroom wall.

"Hey," says I. "What's your guys' names?"

Shaggy boy looks over while freckles climbs up to the top bunk. "I'm Thrasher."

The boy with freckles pushes his blonde hair back for more of a backflow. "I'm Orson."

The four of us introduce ourselves to them.

"What positions do you guys play?" says I.

"I played center for The Dragons," Thrasher says.

"Oh! Why do I feel like I know you?"

"Um, I have no idea."

"What did you play, Orson?"

"I was left wing on Chaska's team," Orson says.

"Same here, bro. Me and Ash are from Kielstad."

"Yeah," Ash says. "We played for the Knights."

"How'd your guys' season go?" Thrasher says.

Me and Ash mirror each other with blank expressions. "Not so great," Ash says.

Thrasher looks at Barrett and Louie. "How bout you guys?"

"We played for Prior Lake," Barrett says. "I'm a right winger."

"I'm left winger," Louie says.

"Dang," says I. "Wouldn't be surprised if some of us have to play center."

"Seriously," Thrasher says. "Looks like we're all wingers in here."

I hear the sound of something ticking. A small red clock hangs above the door. It's half-past eight already. "Looks like we got half an hour till the campfires."

"We should grab our hockey bags, guys," Ash says.

"Oh, shit," Louie says. "Almost forgot about that."

While the other boys start heading out the door, I pull out the picture of me and Chester in our hockey gear. I slide it inside my pillowcase before going outside with the guys.

CAMPFIRE CONNECT

Our hockey bags are stacked in the corner of the room, right in front of my bunk. It's not the biggest deal in the world though. I'm athletic enough to jump off of my bunk. It's the days where I'll be sore from training that might kill me. While I lie on my bed, I listen to the clock tick as I watch a mosquito swarm around our cabin light. I don't like how we're the caboose cabin. It makes me feel frightened that there's nothing on the other side of my wall, everything else is located on the other side of Thrasher's and Orson's wall. Behind my wall is a dark forest where our bus came through. Counselor Campbell also said there were Hunters surrounding the place. I really hope they have night-vision goggles, but it does feel odd to have eyes hiding in the darkness. They can see us, and we can't see them.

"Guys," Louie says. "The campfires start in five minutes. We should get out there."

"Do we have to go?" Ash says. "I'm fricken exhausted from

that bus ride."

"Yes," says I. "We have to."

"Coming from you? I thought you didn't want to meet people."

"I didn't say I didn't want to. I just get anxious about it." Orson peeks his eyes at me from his bunk. "You ready to go, Orson?"

"Yeah," he says.

"Alright," Thrasher says. He whips his hockey cap over his shaggy hair. "Let's get this party started."

I swing my legs over the wooden floor and let them dangle for a second. I slide off and fall to the floor, bending my knees so I don't hurt myself. Barrett and Louie follow Ash out the door. Thrasher grabs his phone and hustles outside. Orson lies in his bed with his eyes shut.

"Orson," says I. "You comin out, man?"

"I don't know," he says.

"Come on out, bud. Counselor Campbell says we have to."

"I'm not feeling well. I just want to sleep right now."

"Are you sure?"

"Yeah. I just need to rest."

"Alright. Suit yourself. Come out if you change your mind." He turns his back to me in bed.

"Are you coming, Liam?" Barrett says.

"I'm coming."

It's cooler outside with shorts and a sweatshirt. Joining up with the others, we make our way to the campfires. There are no signs of any fire. There's not even the stench of burning wood in the air. There's only a cool breeze drifting over the lake and crashing into the woods. The group from Cabin 2 leaves their base and leads the way to the other groups. They're all sitting around dead campfires. Two groups sit around the first campfire, one group sits alone at a different death circle further back, and then there's Cabin 2 and us arriving in time for the meet-n-greet.

"Hello, boys," Counselor Campbell announces. "Find a seat around one of the two campfires. There should be enough bench room for everybody."

Barrett, Louie, Thrasher, Ash, and I find seating spots around the campfire with the one lonely group in the back. The wooden benches are quite nice, but they have a bit of a slant to them. The boys from Cabin 2 sit around the other campfire, which seems to be cramped with guys already. Some of them sit in the grass by the benches while all of their seats are packed, but there are available benches by our campfire. Guess they don't want to sit by us.

"Alright, everyone," Counselor Campbell says. "Quiet down." The side conversations fade out in the breeze. "In half a minute, the fires will ignite. Don't stand anywhere near them when they do. Once they're lit, we'll begin our meet-n-greet."

Barrett sits beside me on the bench. Louie and Ash sit on the other side of him. Thrasher talks to a few guys from Cabin 4 who were sitting here before us. "I thought they were going to light these campfires?" says I.

"I don't know, man," Barrett says. "I just hope it's warm."

"Shame on us. We're Minnesotans. Why are we wanting the

same thing?"

"It gets cold at night sometimes," Barrett says.

"Yeah. I just feel weird complaining about it."

Our ears draw in on a crackling sound from the dead campfire circle. Wood has been prepared into its tipi structure. We watch the wood in the darkness as a spark of light flickers from under the wood. A block lights its own fire. The fire block is like a concrete brick with a thin coating of chalk dust. Suddenly, the fire ignites into blue flames that rise as high as the cafeteria building in the background. All our faces reflect the blue light, and our eyes twinkle in the night sky. I watch the boys around the fire. All of them have their mouths wide open. One of the Cabin 4 members blinds me with his bright smile. He points at the fire and silently chuckles at it.

The fire slowly works its way back down to the burning wood. We all applaud.

"Okay, boys," Counselor Campbell says. "Time for our Campfire Connect. Everyone sitting around your campfire will be introducing themselves to you, and you will be introducing yourselves to them. Say your name, say your position, and tell something interesting about yourself, whether that be a favorite hobby, or maybe even a favorite hockey chirp." Counselor Campbell pulls out a notepad. "Let's see here." Counselor walks over to the crowded campfire first. Finally, the fire turns to its natural yellow. "Ben. Why don't you introduce yourself first?" My vision locks to the other group. My old teammate stands behind the burning wood.

"Ash?" says I. "What the hell is he doing here?"

"I have no idea," he says.

"How didn't we see him? Was he on the bus?"

"Liam, I'm honestly as lost as you are."

"Who are you guys talking about?" Louie asks.

"That guy standing over there," says Ash, "that's our old teammate."

"In high school?"

"Yeah. Ben graduated with us last year."

Ben meets my eyes. He stares for a quick second, then bounces his eyes back to his own group.

Counselor Campbell arrives to our group. "Alright." Don't pick me. Don't pick me. Don't pick me. Please don't pick me. "Liam, you're up first." Frick.

I take a deep breath, then stand on my feet. Everyone's eyes turn to mine. I look into the fire and take another deep breath. My heart beats faster, my arms start twitching, and my shoulders tighten. Just calm down, Liam. Roll your neck around in a circle and just do it. It's a piece of cake. Just get it over with now.

"Hi," says I. "My name is Liam, and I play left wing." Off to the side, I catch Ash's cringey laugh hiding behind Louie's body. "Anyways, I guess one thing that I love is collecting beanie hats. I even snuck one in my luggage to wear, and yes, I'll wear them no matter how hot it is in the summer." I got a few boys to chuckle. I sit down while they clap for me.

Barrett stands from his seat. "I'm Barrett, and I play right wing. I only have one hockey chirp in my head right now, and here it is: It's just like going into the doctor's office . . . When you walk through those doors, you're too weak to take a shot."

Louie's next. "I'm Louie, and I play left wing. A weird fact about me would be that I'm allergic to dusters." The boys hold each other back as they're blown away.

Ash's turn. "I'm Ash, and I play right wing. A fact about me is that I'm joining the military after this camp, and I'm kind of worried about it, but yet I'm excited. I'm ready to break some sticks and bones, and then some more sticks."

Time for the new guys.

The next guy stands up. "My name is Gray, and I play center. My goal is to take away yours." He pulls out a pair of slick shades from his sweats and slides them on. He smiles and high fives the next guy to go.

"I'm Shawn. I play center, as well as Gray does. Yes, my helmet may be a fishbowl, but at least I'm not the one drowning short of breath." Gray holds out another hand for Shawn to slap.

Another boy stands up. He holds up his two pointer fingers together. "My name is Eleven. I play right wing. My favorite chirp: Hey, goalie! This isn't the graveyard shift. Stop digging holes for yourself."

Two boys stand together. They look very identical. They wear the same hockey sweats and shirts, and their bangs flow to the left. Only one of them wears something the other doesn't.

"Hello, everyone. I'm Miles, and this is my brother Max. If you couldn't tell already, we're identical twins. People actually call us the Barrier Boys because we both play defense. The easiest way to split us apart is that I'm the sniper on the ice."

"He's just jealous I have a harder shot," Max says.

"But seriously, the easiest way to tell us apart is that I usually wear this cross necklace, or any sort of necklace or bracelet."

The twins sit back down. Our circle is done.

Thrasher approaches me and squats. "Hey, where's Orson?"

"Um," says I. "He stayed back in the cabin."

"What? I thought he said he was gonna come out?"

"I don't know. He told me he wasn't feeling well."

"Yeah. I've heard that too many times."

"What do you mean?"

"He's shy. He doesn't like to meet new people, nor talk to people for that matter."

"And I thought I was the nervous one."

"You were nervous?"

"Yeah. I'm always nervous when it comes to things like this. I'm able to fight through the anxiety, but it always eats me up. My voice just becomes a shake-quake."

"Well, if you don't mind, maybe you can help me get Orson out of his comfort zone. He can't hide in his cave forever."

"Yes, of course. I can try to help."

"Thanks, Liam."

Thrasher walks back to his bench and chats with slick shade Gray and fishy Shawn. Eleven asks the Barrier Boys questions about identical twin conspiracies, "Can you guys transport thoughts to each other? Have you guys switched spots in school for attendance before? Will you both die at the same age?"

While I want to listen to more conspiracy questions from Eleven, Barrett nudges me on the shoulder. "So, dude. Tell me about that Ben kid."

Oh yeah. I wish he wouldn't be here. "He's just an arrogant first-liner who thinks he's the best of the best."

"Aw. Yep. First-liners can be that way."

"They ARE that way."

"So true. I bet he's one who plays for the show."

"Yes. Oh my God. Finally, someone who's outside of Kielstad that understands."

"Haha. Yeah, it's true though." Our eyes hook on the waving flames. The moon stands tall over the lake now. The breeze feels cooler with every wave passing through the air. "Liam, you seem kind of down lately?"

"Really?"

"Yeah. Are you okay?"

"Yeah, I'm fine."

"Are you sure?"

Down by my feet, the dirt does absolutely nothing. "Well, okay. I've been feeling down for a while, but it's nothing new."

"Well, what are you feeling down about?"

"It's just . . . my friend, Chester, the one in the picture that I dropped on the bus, I've been missing him lately. I've been missing him a lot."

"Sorry, bro." He pats me on the back. "I didn't mean to bring that up."

"No, no. It's fine. I should probably talk it out anyway. I've been in a down mood for a few months now. I thought it would get easier, but it doesn't."

"Dude, I'm going through the same thing as you, I mean, not the same situation, but I've been in the dumps for years now. My parents lost our home in the financial crisis. We had to move to a house and rent it for a year, but then after that, we decided to move in with my grandparents. But before I left . . . Grandma threatened my mom and I saw my mom cry—" Barrett's eyes flood up. They shimmer in the burning light. "I've been watching my parents in a depression for years." Gross. My head can never seem to handle that word. I don't even want to think about it. I'm not one of those people. "I never want to go back."

I settle a hand around his back for comfort. He wipes his eyes and sets his chin down on his supporting hand. The light flashes on our faces. "I'll always be here for you, Barrett. I know we just met and all, but there's always a home for you at my place. I know that's probably not what you want but—"

"That's definitely what I want. I don't want to see my parents again."

"Aw, Barrett. I don't think you mean that, bud."

"I just can't think anymore. I feel so lost. It's like I'm floating in space and I can see all of the stars, but nothing is in reach. I just can't find my feelings anymore."

"Touché."

Counselor Campbell hops onto a wooden bench. "Alright, boys. That'll do for the night. Tomorrow morning, you'll have brunch, and then you'll get to meet the Commander of Camp

59

Kelmo at the Grotto. Remember, you need to stay indoors till sunrise. Head off now to get some rest, boys. Training begins in two days."

"We'll have to take a walk together sometime," Barrett says.

"Deal," says I.

Back at our cabins, we tuck in for the night. I hop on my bunk and forget the thought of brushing my teeth. My eyes are heavy, and my mouth is dry like sand that's been sitting in the scorching sunlight. Orson's back is facing me again. I don't know if he's really asleep or not, but me and Barrett will have to help him out. But in the meantime, I'll have to see if I can sleep or not. Ben's face keeps popping up inside of my head. It's like living in a nightmare.

GROTTO

Sweet cinnamon rolls swirl in the Cafeteria, and the chitter-chatter spreads around the room like peanut butter on toast. The rooms quite large for just thirty people, but at least Counselor Campbell makes us all sit together in the two columns of tables. A cafeteria lady sets a giant cinnamon roll on my brunch tray. I grab the frosting tube and flood the top of it with white, gooey lava. I move down the line behind Ash. I take an apple from the fruit basket, a mini cardboard container of chocolate milk, and a small bowl of vanilla yogurt and granola.

I stroll in between the two long and busy lunch tables, finding my cabin members at the end on the left. I sit on the table's bench as my saliva melts to the cinnamon roll. Barrett, Louie, and Orson sit across from me. Ash plops a seat on my right, and behind him comes Thrasher. To my left are the new guys we met last night. Gray discovers the frosting on his cinnamon roll dripped down his whole forearm. Fishbowl Shawn takes his arm and pretends to lick it off. Gray slaps his hand away. Max and Miles consume their food in peace at the far end of the table. Eleven stands in line with some of the other players, waiting for their food.

I mush the cinnamon roll in my mouth. The lava frosting seeps between my teeth as the cinnamon and bread dissolve on my tongue. I continue to chew on the soft fluff while I prop my carton of chocolate milk open.

Ash pours chocolate milk in his mouth. He raises his head and gargles back on the milk. "Ash," says I.

He finishes gargling, then he sends me a smile. I shove him on the shoulder in acceptance of his personality.

"These cinnamon rolls are so good," says I. I dive in deep with another bite.

"Honestly," Louie says. "These are the bomb."

Orson eats his with a fork. He keeps his head down.

"How's your cinnamon roll, Orson?" says I.

"Fine," he says. Me and Barrett exchange looks. He shrugs his shoulders at me.

"Are we training today?" Thrasher says.

"Tomorrow," Ash says.

"What are we doing today again?"

"Meeting with the Commander."

"Commander?"

"Uh huh."

"Didn't know we were in a military camp."

Ash chuckles. "I know right. Didn't know I was trying out for the military so soon."

"Dude," Louie says. "I don't think I could ever face that challenge."

"The military?" Ash says.

"Yeah. That's some fricken intense training right there."

"I just hope I'm buff after it all."

"What are you talking about?" says I. "You're fricken buff already!"

"But like I want to be buffer."

"You're a beast."

"We're both beasts." Me and Ash twist to each other and chest bump.

"What the hell?" Thrasher says.

"What?" says I.

"Why did you guys do that?"

"In high school, we were known as The Beasts."

"We were the toughest line out on the ice," Ash says. "We'd continually knock out guys."

"Those were the days," says I. "I look forward to doing it again in the future, or at least I hope we can figure it out."

"We will. Don't worry. After I come home from deployment and you have time from college, we can join a league together."

"I don't even know what college I want to go to."

"But you know what you want to do, right?"

"Not anymore. Film school was my first option."

"Oh," Louie says. "If you write a story, you should name me after one of your characters."

"Me too," Thrasher says.

"And me," Ash says.

"I'll make sure to keep that in my notes."

An air horn blasts across the room. Counselor Campbell stands at the end of the tables. "Mornin, boys," he says. "I hope your breakfast has suited you well. If you're not finished with your food, scuff it down. We will be heading outside to the Grotto. It's time to meet your Commander. On your way out, set your trays in two piles at the end of your table. Let's move."

We all flip our legs around our benches and stand. I stretch before taking my tray to the tray pile. We follow the others outside. Counselor Campbell leads us down the lakeside. At the end, a gigantic rock grotto caves over a staging area. A marble podium stands at the end of the rocky stage. The Grotto curls over the podium like snake fangs. Deep inside the Grotto is a cave leading into the darkness.

We stop in front of the towering podium. Counselor Campbell walks up steps that were naturally formed by the eroding rock stage. He reaches the top and stays off to the side. I can hear the drip-drips dropping down from the wet grass above the Grotto. The morning dew must be drying out. The sun peeks behind a cloud and strikes its heat on us. It's already hot enough with all of us bunched up together. If there's anything I hate, it's standing and waiting.

Heels click and echo from the cave. Two guys walk out in dark green suits, they carry loaded crossbows. A badge sticks on their sleeves. The symbol on the badge is an owl twisting its neck around, staring at you with its two bulging eyes. Their shirts are buttoned up all the way to the top. They wear boots which cover in mucky mud. On top of their heads, they wear a hat that mimics a budenovka; a hat used in the Russian military with floppy ears and a round tip. I remember playing a video game on the console based around the Cold War, and the animated Russians were wearing those vintage hats. These guys, these two monstrous guys, are Hunters.

The Hunters turn away from each other and split to the sides of the Grotto stage. From behind the podium, a woman with straightened, brown hair approaches. She clicks her heels up to the podium and stands under the snake fangs. All of us wait in silence.

"Greetings," the woman says. "Welcome to Camp Kelmo! I'm Commander Moriz. I will be leading you guys on your journey of this very special opportunity. You boys will learn to build strengths in several categories that will help you in your future hockey careers. But before I go in-depth with the camp, Counselor Campbell has done a wonderful job with you guys. Give him a round of applause." We clap and cheer for Counselor Campbell. He raises his hand in the air. Of course, one of the guys whistles. There's always a person in a crowd that seems to know how to whistle with their fingers these days. "Counselor Campbell will make sure you all keep disciplined around the camp. You boys will be meeting with your coaches tonight. Teams have been divided equally. Each team will have fifteen players. Cabins 1 and 2 will unite as one, and Cabins 4 and 5 will team up together. Cabin 3 will be cut down the line with three guys joining each side." Some of the boys start looking around at each other. I meet eyes with Ben again, then I pretend that I didn't see him and look around at the other guys. "Your team training starts tomorrow. Before you boys step inside of The Burg and train on ice, you'll be training on dry land. Dryland consists of team building, team versus team competitions, and individual challenges. Make sure you boys are ready for tomorrow. It's time to train and gain."

The boys applaud Commander Moriz as she walks back into the Grotto's cave. The two Hunters follow her inside. Counselor Campbell steps up to the podium.

"Boys," he says. "Till seven o'clock, you boys may do as you wish around the camp. You must stay off the surrounding hills. There's a path that follows around the backside of the lake if you want to hike, and the sandy beach by the dock is open for swimming. Just make sure you boys behave. Make sure you're cleaned up and ready to meet your coaches tonight."

He walks off stage. The boys all disperse, but Ash and the others approach me in a circle. Counselor Campbell passes by and heads to the Training Office.

"Do you guys wanna go swimming?" Thrasher says.

"Oh my God," Ash says. "Yes."

"It's getting quite hot," Louie says.

Me and Barrett nod at each other. "We're in," Barrett says. He pats Orson on the shoulder. Orson glares at Barrett.

We head to the cabins for our swimming gear as the humidity sticks to the stones.

SPLASH WARS

I tightly tie my trunks around my waist in our cabin's bathroom. My trunks are red with black horizontal stripes; I'm usually never picky when I shop for new clothes. Mom always makes me go clothes shopping once in a while, but she's always wanting me to buy more "dressy" clothes. I never find jeans to be comfortable, and I've always disliked those flat skater shoes. Tennis and hiking shoes are the only good shoes around for my feet.

My feet mix in colors from the burns last year like paint splatters on a blank canvas. The doctor said that my feet would heal, but they won't look the same. Sometimes, it still hurts to touch the burns. My shower water can only be luke-warm, and it cannot go any higher. I'll find myself in a strange stance where I put pressure on my foot with my other foot, and it feels like poles impaling through them. I'm always discovering new ways to hurt myself these days.

I heap my left foot up on the kitchen sink and look at its sole through the mirror. Skin peels around the dark burns like a shedding snake. I really don't want my friends seeing my feet, but I don't think there's anything to cover it up. I'll leave my shirt on though to cover up the little belly fat I have. All the other kids around here have bread rolls on their stomach, I just know it. I wish I can look and have the confidence like them, but no matter how much time I spend at the gym, nothing seems to be improving. Hopefully, this camp can help me out.

The wooden door shakes from behind me. "Hold on," says I. I turn around with my clothes, unlock the door, and open it. Ash stands there with his trunks.

"Finally," he says.

"I wasn't taking that long."

He slams the door shut. I bring my clothes over to my bunk and throw them on my bed. Orson sits on Thrasher's bed. Thrasher and Louie are swimming in the lake already with some of the other guys. Barrett lies in bed with his trunks on. He looks through his phone but then puts it to sleep. He searches for something in between his mattress and the wall.

"Do you guys know where the outlets are?" Barrett says.

"No," says I. I help search, but no outlets seem apparent in the cabin. "I'm not seeing any."

"Maybe there's one in the bathroom." Barrett knocks on the bathroom door.

"I'll be out in a sec," Ash says.

"Do you see an outlet in there?"

"No. I couldn't find one last night either."

Barrett tosses his phone on his bed. "Guess we won't have our phones."

"Maybe there are some in the cafeteria," says I.

"I hope so."

Ash pushes the door open and walks out. "Let's go swimming!" he says.

"Yes," Barrett says. "Let's do this."

They grab their towels and run out the screened-in door. Every guy has their shirt off, even a guy who's chubbier than me. I rip my shirt off and throw it on my bed. Orson's still as a stone on Thrasher's bed, right next to his folded-up towel.

"Come on, Orson," says I.

Orson grabs his towel and follows me out of the cabin. We walk down the steps and cross the grassy road. The hard dirt ground transitions to a plush pillow of sand. We kick the sand back as we trudge our way to the water. We find an open spot to lay our towels down in the baking sun.

"Maybe I should've brought sunscreen," says I. "Don't wanna get burnt." Orson kneels down on his towel and lays on his back. "You gonna come swimming with me?" He stares at the dancing leaves from one of the trees off to the side. I kneel down on my towel and look out to find Louie, Barrett, Thrasher, and Ash having a splash war. Fishbowl Shawn and Eleven swim over and join them in the chaos. "Hey. I know you probably don't like meeting new people, and I'm definitely with ya on that. I have anxiety in certain situations, and when it comes to meeting kids the same age as me, I don't know why, but it takes a toll on my emotions. But I think it would be best if we both go out in the water together."

"Thanks, Liam" he says. "It means a lot."

"No problem, bud. Let's go jump in then."

"Wait, Liam. I can't go swimming."

"What do you mean?"

"I literally can't go. I can't swim."

"You don't know how to swim?"

"No. The water has always scared me since I was a kid."

"You should be fine sticking in the shallow area though. The boys won't go too far. That would be too much of a workout."

Orson gives in a little smile. "I don't know."

"Trust me. You'll do fine."

Orson evaluates the shoreline with the guys splashing around. "Okay. I'll go out."

"Yay! Let's sneak up behind and splash them all."

Me and Orson sprint on the sand, kicking it up from the ground and making dust clouds. Our feet crash into the water as we span our arms out and fall into a splash. The water slaps the guys across the face. Louie and Thrasher turn around and splash us right back. I close my eyes and hold my breath through the walls of water crashing into me. Once their arms die out, I blow the water out that went up my nose and proceed to splash the others. Orson joins and splashes with me in the waist-deep water.

After some time passes while swimming, I find Barrett staring out across the lake and into the woods. I follow his path of sight and see three of the boys on the hiking trail. "Hey," says I.

"What you thinkin about?"

"Home," Barrett says. "I'm thinking about home."

"Are you homesick already?"

"No. I guess I'm thinking about my parents more than anything."

The water surrounds our necks as we submerged our shoulders under the surface. We keep looking out across the round lake. "I haven't told you yet, but my father died in an accident before my first high school hockey game."

"What?" he says. "Dude, I'm so sorry to hear that."

"Thanks, Barrett. He never got to watch me play in high school, but I always wonder how different it would be if he was still alive."

"I couldn't even imagine, dude."

"Yeah. I can't seem to imagine it either, but I can't stop thinking about it."

"You know, I think things happen in life for a reason, and I know a lot of people say that, but like, every tiny thing happens for a reason. Ya know? Like my parents are suffering in a depression right now and it sucks, but yet I end up here and I'm actually feeling a little like me again."

"That's what we do. We find our love and use it as an escape pod from our sinking ship."

"True that."

"Hockey's life, and I don't know what I'd do without it. I guess looking back to it all, all those years of suffering, what if everything in the past was the same but we didn't have hockey on our side?"

"I couldn't even imagine life," Barrett says. "I'd probably be having suicidal thoughts."

"You think so?"

"Yeah, I mean, it seems like a normal human thing to do while living in something you can't get out of. I'm forced to watch my parents argue every day for entertainment and eat depression for meals."

"Yeah. I can't imagine hockey not being a part of our lives."

"It's family."

"Cheers to that."

The other boys exit the water and dry off in their sandy towels. "Must be time," says I.

"Yeah," Barrett says. "Time to clean up and meet our coaches."

We push through the water and make it to the shoreline. The warm breeze blows on our backs while the hot sand sticks to our feet like glitter to glue. I shake the sand off my towel. Orson hops off of his towel and shakes it as well.

We walk off the beach with our sandy feet and to our cabin. The time has come to meet our summer coaches.

COACHES

We chill on our bunk beds while the stars sprinkle in the sky. The heat has dissipated while the cooler air seeps inside the cabin. Crickets cricket in the background, and a couple of mosquitos fly around the light again. The clock points to seven. A whistle blares through the screened-in windows. Two men stand outside, each one holding a fire-lit lamp. More whistles come from further away.

Thrasher stands and looks outside. "Coaches are here."

Our cabin walks outside and down the steps. Gray, Shawn, Eleven, some kid I haven't met, and the Barrier Brothers, Max and Miles, exit next door from Cabin 4. Both our cabins circle up in front of the coaches. Two more random guys walk over to our group from Cabin 3.

"Welcome, boys," one of the coaches says. "I'm Coach Hill. I'll be your head coach for the summer."

The other coach steps in. He wears a black lab coat which

goes to his knees, black lab pants, and clear glasses. He presses a button on his clear glasses. The clear plastic shines a light blue which pops his eyes out. "I'm Dr. Fallenhein. I'll be keeping track of your guys' training results. So basically, you can look at me as your assistant coach."

"We are happy to be coaching for you guys," Coach Hill says. "The big day kicks off tomorrow. If you haven't already noticed, your team is made up of Cabins 4 and 5, but we also had to split Cabin 3 in half to make both teams even. And I'm sure you boys from 4 and 5 have met each other already, so I'll just briefly introduce the new guys." Coach Hill gestures his hand at two boys in the back with short, bleached-looking hair. "This is Eli and Viktor. They're a defensive pair that traveled all the way from Russia to be here with us." We give them a round of applause. Coach Hill checks around the group but ends in confusion. "Where's our third guy from Cabin 3?"

Louie points to the chubbier kid who swam in the lake earlier. "Isn't this him? We haven't met each other yet."

"No. He's from Cabin 4. This is your goalie, Siv." I can't help but chuckle with a few others.

"I know, I know," Siv says. "It hit me hard in middle school when I actually understood what my name meant."

"Anyways," Dr. Fallenhein says, "While we figure out the confusion, you guys will begin team training tomorrow. There are three challenges you guys will be going through: team training, team versus team, and individual. These challenges will help us gain results before you boys step on the ice. We'll conduct the research and see what we can do to improve your skills."

"Team training will start at one tomorrow. You guys will meet us at the beach over there. Make sure you get some good rest tonight."

Coach Hill and Doctor Fallenhein leave. As we all hop back in our cabins, I look at the other guys from Cabins 1 and 2. They're all cheering and clapping. I notice Ben walking up the steps to Cabin 1. That's his cabin. He claps his hands like he's trying to lure a dog over to him.

I enter the cabin and flush the door shut. We all hop back in our beds and hide under our blankets. I begin to doze off to some of the boys' soft conversations. My eyes droop down, and the light fades out. I take a deep breath in, then a deep breath out.

Slam! I throw my upper body out of my bed and find myself in the dark. The light's off in the cabin, and the guys are all sleeping. The moon shines high in the night sky, and the moon's reflection from the lake bounces the cold light into our cabin. I can barely read the time on the clock. It's around the devil's hour.

While a mosquito wizzes around my head, a soft whimpering sound seeps through. I hear it from the other side of my bunk. Barrett moves to his side and faces the wall from his top bunk. He's silently crying.

I crawl out of my sheets and over to Barrett's bed. I go on the outside of him as he makes room for me. He flips on his other side to face me.

"I can't do it," Barrett says. "I can't sleep."

"What's wrong, Barrett?" says I. "Tell me."

"I just can't anymore."

"Can't what?"

"I'm depressed. After all this time of suffering, I've been lying to myself. I'm not fine. I'm fucking depressed."

Barrett's eyes reflect the light bouncing in from the lake. The light shimmers upon the ponds in his eyes. I flush my ponds out with Barrett. Dad comes to mind, and all those memories with him on the ice, and those road trips we took together up north. I wish he was still alive. "I've lied to myself too. I wish I could see my dad again." Me and Barrett flood our tears out in the sheets. I reach an arm over him, giving him a gentle hug. He does the same for me.

We drain our ponds and drift asleep.

CANOE CROSS

Directly after lunch, we leave the cafeteria and meet at the beach. We circle around Coach Hill and Dr. Fallenhein who stand at the edge of the sand. The water's calm today, but the sun isn't bursting down its rays. Grey clouds blanket the sky. The humidity's here, sticking to the skin like maple syrup. From behind the coaches, I see Ben's team grouped up in a bunch. They're more talkative than our team seems to be. They push each other around while their coaches try and gain their attention.

"Boys," Coach Hill says. "Welcome to team training." Coach Hill signals Dr. Fallenhein. Dr. Fallenhein grabs a red gym bag from the ground. It's full of blue t-shirts. He pries the bag open, loosening the white strings as they dangle off to the side. He tosses them out to us. A shirt flies in my direction. I jump in the air and snatch it before anyone else can. All the shirts appear to be a men's large, which is perfect for me, I guess. On the backside of the blue t-shirt, it reads Camp Kelmo. I flip the shirt around to the front side, and in a shattering ice-blue, it reads Team Frost. "Welcome to Team Frost. You'll be challenging Team Ink for the summer. This first challenge will require teamwork. You'll need to learn to work with your teammates through communicating. You'll have to solve problems together. There's nothing more important to a team than its chemistry." He steps back and gestures Dr. Fallenhein.

"Well, this is one exciting day, isn't it?" Dr. Fallenhein says. He's wearing his black lab jacket and pants again. I really hope he has more than one pair. He holds up a clipboard and reads it through his clear glasses. "Today, you'll be paddling in the canoe cross. You'll be split into three groups. There'll be three canoes on your team, five guys in each one. Four of you will paddle, and one of you will direct. You will not be racing Team Ink. Your goal is to make it to the other side of the lake with your trio. Stay together, support one another, and you'll be on your way to success."

The two coaches from Team Ink blow their whistles as the boys commence onto the dock.

"Let's go, boys!" Coach Hill says. He blows his whistle. We commence to the dock where canoes are tied to the wooden supports. On the left side of the dock, Team Ink fills their three canoes. We take the three canoes on the right.

Gray, wearing his backwards hockey cap, runs to the front canoe with Thrasher. Louie and the Barrier Brothers join them in the front. It's finally easy to tell Miles from Max since he wears his dangling cross around his neck.

Fishbowl Shawn and Eleven hop into the middle canoe. They take the back seats and grab their paddles in a hurry. The new Russians from Cabin 3, Eli and Viktor, take the open seats in front of them.

"We need one more person," Eleven yells.

One of the kids from Team Ink yells, "Shut up!"

"How bout you shut down, fucker!" Eleven receives a high-five from Shawn.

Ash turns to me. "I'll hop in with them."

"Are you sure?" says I.

"Yeah. It'll be fine. I'll make sure they're staying on task." He leaps into the canoe.

The back canoe is mine. I lunge off the dock and sit in the front. Guess that means I'll be the director. Siv sits down behind me and grabs a side paddle. Barrett and Orson stare at the backbench together.

"Let's hop in the back seat," Barrett says.

While Barrett gets inside the canoe, Orson freezes up and stares at it while it rocks in the water. Barrett finds him frozen like a statue.

"Orson," Barrett says. "What's wrong?"

"Where are the lifejackets?" he says. He shivers while rubbing his hands down his arms, trying to keep calm as the lake.

Coach Hill notices Orson. He's the last one standing on the dock. "What's wrong, kid?" Orson still stares at the dark water beneath the canoe.

"Do you have lifejackets?" Barrett says.

"No lifejackets. He'll be fine."

"Can you swim?" Barrett asks. Orson's teeth rattle. Barrett stands in the canoe and reaches a hand. Orson reaches out for Barrett's hand, then he takes it slow, moving one foot inside the canoe's bellow. He grabs the wooden support and sets his other foot inside. Barrett helps him sit while the canoe sways in the water.

Siv checks around the dock. "Um," he says. "Coach?"

"What?" Coach Hill says.

"We're missing a guy."

"What do you mean?"

"Ugh. We're missing a human being."

"Well, who's not here?"

I scan the other canoes. "I think we're all here, coach," says I.

"Do you think, or do you know?"

"I know. We have everyone from our team. Remember? We only had two cabin members from Cabin 3 the other night."

"Well, what the fuck!" Coach Hill yells. One thing's for sure, never correct a coach. He investigates the canoes on Team Ink. The back two canoes have five guys inside. The front canoe contains six.

"It's fine, coach," Barrett says. "We can do it without one."

"You guys will be outnumbered for the rest of the summer."

"One guy won't make a difference for us. We're up for the challenge."

Coach Hill wants a response from Dr. Fallenhein, but he shrugs. Eli and Viktor are from Cabin 3, and one guy from that cabin didn't follow his order. That one fricken guy stuck with his clicky friends on Team Ink.

Coach walks on the dock as the wood creaks from under his heavy steps. He points at one of the kids in the canoe of six. "Hop in that canoe for Team Frost, just this one time." A kid in black exits the canoe. I can't believe it. What are the odds that coach would pick the most lethal poison in this camp to help us? Ben gives me a long stare with his jaw clenched shut while he walks behind coach on the creaky dock. He jumps inside, shaking the canoe like we're riding on ocean waves. Orson slides to Barrett as the water splashes at him.

The sound of heels approaches closer and closer behind us. Commander Moriz struts the wooden dock and walks to the end of it. She turns around and looks at us with smiling, puckered-up lips. "Welcome to your first training course, boys. I wish you all luck in your challenges. While this is the first of many challenges, I'll be sending you off on your voyage." Her pristine teeth shine as she models them off. "Let's begin."

The coaches in the back blow their whistles. The guys in front of me untie the ropes to their canoes. I turn around and look at my crew. Barrett and Ben loosen the ropes and toss them into the water.

Thrasher stands high in the front canoe. "Travel in a triangle!" he yells back.

Ash stands from his middle canoe. "We'll take left."

"Okay," says I. "We'll take right."

Thrasher's canoe paddles away. Me and Ash direct our

canoes to make the bottom of the triangle. He takes the left side as we'll paddle to the right.

"Alright," says I. "Even it out now. We don't want to crash into our own team."

Team Ink forms their canoes in a wall. They're moving ahead of us. "Can we paddle any faster?" Ben says.

"This isn't about racing," says I.

"No, but I'd like to get this over with."

"This isn't your team."

"I didn't want to be on your team in the first place."

"Good. You aren't. You're only helping us for one challenge, and then you can be back with your cool friends again." Ben stops paddling. The canoe moves to the right. We begin to swerve away from our triangle. I jolt my head around to find Ben not paddling. "What are doing?"

"Liam," Ash says. "Keep up."

"Ben," says I. "We need to stay with our group."

"You mean your group," he says. "You're the captain now. Figure it out."

Ash yells to Thrasher out front, "Thrasher. Stop."

While Team Ink zips across the lake in their wall, our team stalls near the middle of the lake. Our canoes are about a quarter of the way across. Ben holds us all up.

"What the fuck is happening?" Thrasher yells.

I point at Ben. "This kid won't help us."

"Dude," Thrasher says to Ben. "Come on. This isn't cool."

Siv glances at him. "Seriously, man."

Ben glares at me again.

"Come on," Thrasher says. "Daylights burning."

Ben picks up the paddle and smacks it at the lake. The water splashes back at Barrett's face, drenching him from top to bottom.

"Really, dude," Barrett says. "I just got this shirt."

Ben drops the paddle in the canoe again and turns around. He punches Barrett in the jaw. Barrett falls back but catches himself on the back of the canoe. I stumble to the back as the canoe sways from side to side. Some of the water whips over the edge and inside of the canoe. I pull Ben away from Barrett, but he throws me back into the front. My head clanks against the steel floor. Siv shoves Ben down into his seat.

I get on my feet and tower over Ben. "Ben," says I. "The past is behind us now. Stop acting like a mini mite and paddle."

Thrasher yells over to Ash, "Are they situated now?"

"I think so," Ash says.

Our canoe begins to sink backwards. Orson turns around and feels the imbalance. He slides over to Barrett. Barrett hugs him. "It's okay, Orson," Barrett says. The canoe continues to sink down like the Titanic, but no water leaks inside. Ash and Thrasher start feeling the sinking sensation too from their canoes.

"What is that?" Thrasher says.

"I have no idea," Ash says.

Suddenly, our canoes go crashing forward into the water. I fall down with my hair dipping into the grey lake water. The canoe creaks as a circular wave moves to the center of the lake. Ash and Thrasher sit on their seats again and watch the waves close in on each other. The circular wave flushes underwater.

A huge machine shoots out from the lake's pupil. A huge circular wave rolls into action, and it's heading right for us.

"Move out!" Ash yells.

"Go!" Thrasher yells. "Go! Go! Go!"

The huge wave crashes into Thrasher's and Ash's canoe. The canoe flips them upside down and submerges them underwater. Orson squeezes onto Barrett and hides his eyes into his chest. The wave towers over us.

"Hang on!" says I.

Our canoe rises up the surf's wave. I close my eyes as the water sprays at my face. We reach a ninety-degree vertical, and I find myself squeezing onto the sides of the canoe for life. The wave crashes down on us. I splash into the water and barrel-roll. The bubbles fizz around my ears. I plop my eyes open, but the bubbles fly around me like a swarm of hornets. As I intake water through my nose, I see the bright grey light from the overcast sky. I swim towards the top as I feel the waves flex the surface. I kick and kick and kick till I finally pull myself out to the surface. I gasp for air and wipe the water from my eyes. I look around for the others, but the waves make it tough. I see Ash's crew flipping their canoe over, and Thrasher's crew is retrieving theirs. I spin around and find our canoe floating upside down. Siv and Ben swim over to it and push it over on its base.

Barrett splashes out from afar. "Liam!" Barrett yells. He gags on water. "Help!" Orson latches his hands onto Barrett's shoulders and pushes him underwater.

I propel myself through the water. "Orson!" says I. "Stop!" I try to yell again as I continue to make my way over, but I gag in the waves. Barrett raises his head out from the water and takes a deep breath. Orson submerges him again. I reach to Orson as he jumps onto me. He shoves me underwater.

Barrett gasps for air. "Orson," he says. "Wrap an arm around me." Orson takes his right arm and wraps it around Barrett's shoulder. I kick back to the surface and grasp for all the air I can get. Orson wraps his other arm around me and continues to kick his feet like a dog.

"It's okay, Orson," says Barrett. "We got you."

"We need to get back on that canoe," says I. "Now."

We swim to the canoe where Ben stands on Sivs' shoulders. He leaps off of him and falls inside of the canoe. Siv plunges underwater for a second but resurfaces. Ben reaches out for Orson's hand and helps us pull him into the canoe. Orson lays on the canoe's steel floor and starts crying. Barrett uses his feet to push off of my shoulders while Ben pulls him in.

"How am I going to get in?" Siv says. "I'm too heavy."

"We'll figure it out," says I.

"No. I'll capsize the boat."

From above, Ben towers over me. "Alright," says I. "Here's what we're gonna do. Barrett, Orson, you two will row the canoe together, keeping us on a straight path. Ben, you'll lead our way back to shore. Siv and I will head to the back and push." Siv nods.

"Orson," Barrett says. "Come on, bud. I need you." Orson crawls next to Barrett. Barrett reaches into the water on the other side of the canoe and grabs one of the floating paddles. The other three were in the canoe already; Ben and Siv must've thrown them on while we were helping Orson. "Alright, we're gonna start paddling." Me and Siv clutch on the back of the canoe and push. Ash's and Thrasher's crew made it on their canoes and wait for us to form our triangle again. We begin to make our way across the lake, crossing over the giant circle machine that created the wave. The machine slowly sinks down into the depths, dissolving into the reflection of the overcast clouds.

When we make it to the other side of the lake, Team Ink is exiting out of the water. Most of them are drenched from head to toe like they've been playing in a downpour. They look back at our canoes and watch us in silence. Me and Siv touch the mucky ground as our feet sink in the quicksand. Our team hops out of the canoes, pulling them onto the wooded shoreline. Coach Hill and Dr. Fallenhein appear behind the trees on the hiking path. Team Ink's coaches enter from the other side of the trail.

"Way to go, Team Frost," Coach Hill says.

"What the hell was that?" Thrasher says.

"Your team's challenge."

"We almost fucking died out there."

"Watch your language."

"Don't tell me what to do."

Dr. Fallenhein budges in front of Coach Hill. "Is anyone hurt?" he says. No responses. "Alright then. Nothing to complain about."

"Are you serious?" Thrasher yells.

"Thrasher," Gray says. He attempts to pull Thrasher out of the conversation. "Stop."

"No. Someone almost died on our team."

"Boys," Coach Hill says. "Back to your cabins, now."

Thrasher gives coach the finger. He stomps down the trail with Gray following behind him. Everyone else begins to walk down the long trail. Ben steps aside from our team, giving a glorious glare to me, then moves back to Team Ink.

While the trees stand still, I get a move on with my team.

INTRUSION

I lounge on my bed with my other cabin members. Thrasher lies on his bottom bunk, throwing a bouncy ball in the air and catching its fall. Orson is above him, sitting straight up in bed with applesauce legs. Behind me, Barrett chills in bed with his dead phone sitting beside him. All our phones are dead by now. We still haven't been able to find charging ports anywhere. Louie chills in his bed, probably trying to take a nap. I bend over the edge of my bed and see Ash stretching his legs.

My arms are floppy like croppies. Swimming makes my arms feel so weak, but then they turn out worse the following day. That makes total sense why coaches don't want us swimming in pools before games, but it doesn't make sense why coaches would burn our legs before gameday either. I shouldn't complain though. It keeps us in shape. It keeps me in shape.

The screened-in door slams open. Coach Hill juts in with two Hunters behind him. They have their crossbows at rest. Coach carries an empty, marble chest.

"Put your phones in the chest," he says. "All of you." Orson shivers at the sight of the black crossbow, loaded with an arrow ready to fire. Ash turns around and finds Louie staring at him. Barrett looks down at his dead phone. "I want all of your phones in this crate, now."

Barrett jumps off of his bunk. He grabs his dead phone and places it in the marble chest. Next, Louie places his phone in the chest. Me and Ash go together and set our phones inside. Coach Hill looks at the last two in the room; Orson and Thrasher. Orson's teeth rattle, drawing in Coach Hill. He moves over to him and raises the box. Orson slides his phone out from his pocket and gently places it on the others. Coach smiles. He squats down in front of Thrasher with the chest.

"I didn't bring mine with," Thrasher says.

"Your mother didn't let you bring your phone to camp?" Coach Hill says.

"Actually, it was my dad who wouldn't let me bring it with."

"Oh. Well isn't that so." Coach steps back in front of the Hunters. "Search him."

The closest Hunter marches over to him, almost stabbing Thrasher in the face with the arrowhead of the bow. He searches Thrasher's pockets finding nothing inside. The other Hunter walks over to Thrasher and reaches out to pick him up.

"No!" Thrasher says. "Don't touch me." The Hunter lifts Thrasher out from his bed.

The other Hunter throws the sheets off and searches under his mattress. Nothing. The Hunter shakes the pillow and feels around the pillowcase. Still nothing.

"Where's your phone?" Coach Hill says.

"I don't have it," Thrasher says.

The Hunter holding him scratches him with the blade of the arrowhead. Thrasher wimps.

"Stop!" says I. "You're hurting him."

"Where's your phone?" Coach Hill says.

"I don't have it," Thrasher says.

"We aren't getting anywhere with this," Coach Hill says. "Take him."

"No. Please!" The Hunters follow Coach Hill out the door with Thrasher in their hands.

"What are you doing with him?" says I.

"Liam!" Thrasher yells.

We watch the Hunters steal Thrasher from our cabin. Orson cries. I turn around. Barrett's as lost as me.

"What's happening, guys?" Louie says.

"We're in military training," Ash says. "I didn't know I'd be starting so soon."

"Are you serious?" Louie asks.

"Hold on a sec," says I. "This isn't military camp."

"Did you see him take Thrasher away?" Ash says. "Did you forget what happened at the lake?"

"Look, I know this all seems different, but we need to calm down."

"Calm down? Are you kidding me?"

"It's our first day of training."

"And we could've died."

"We have other training days to go. Let's just see where this takes us."

Ash shuts up. If there's one thing I don't want to lose this year, it's my sport of hockey. After we graduated high school, hockey was taken away from me. I was lucky enough to have been invited to this camp. I'm not letting the opportunity slip away, especially if it means I get a second chance of being scouted to a junior's team.

Ash pushes himself out of bed and stomps his feet to the screened-in door. He turns the handle of the door, but the door doesn't budge open. He attempts to open it again, but it doesn't move. He takes a few steps back, then charges the door. When he checks the door with his shoulder, he bounces back and slams onto the floor. A blue forcefield traps us inside. It shimmers around the door and windows.

"Do you see that, Liam?" Barrett says.

"I do," says I.

Orson shoves his head into his pillow, pouring out his tears. I hop off my bed and jump onto Orson's. I lay beside him and wrap my arm around his shoulders.

THE BURG

The morning rain cools the summer air. The drops pitter-patter on the cabin's roof. The leaves soak up the falling tears as a strike of lightning flickers in the dark sky. Thunder rumbles the ground, waking the other guys. I lift my chest and turn to Orson's bunk. Thrasher isn't there.

"Thrasher's not back?" Louie says.

"I never saw him walk in," Ash says.

The wooden floor creaks louder and louder with footsteps. Dr. Fallenhein enters our cabin with a plate of frosted cinnamon rolls and a gallon of milk. We all jump out of our sheets and scurry over to him, everyone besides Orson. I steal two cinnamon rolls from the plate, handing one to Orson.

"Thanks," Orson says. I smile back.

"Meet outside by the campfires when you're done," Dr. Fallenhein says. He hands the gallon of milk to Ash as he scuffs down the cinnamon roll in one bite. Dr. Fallenhein leaves.

I chew on my gushy cinnamon roll. The white lava soaks into my taste buds. The sweet cinnamon swirls in the cabin. Ash swallows his roll, then he opens the gallon of milk and chugs. When he finishes, he hands it to Barrett and Louie. After they take their swigs, I gulp down the cold dairy and leave a good remainder of it for Orson.

"Are you sure?" Orson says.

"Yeah," says I. "Finish it off." He smiles, then chugs the rest. "I guess we should go outside."

"Yeah," Ash says. He marches to the door. "Can't wait." He slams the door shut behind him.

"What's his problem?" Louie says.

"I don't know," says I.

"Nervous," Barrett says. "Nervous like the rest of us."

He's not completely wrong. I'm not nervous about the training though, but I am nervous for Thrasher. I don't know where he went. I don't know what they're doing with him. I don't know if he's coming back. And now, we don't have our phones. The camp took away our only way of communicating with the outside world.

We head out of Cabin 5 to the campfires in the downpour. Our team stands in front of Dr. Fallenhein and Coach Hill. Team Ink stands around their coaches by another firepit. As we approach our group, I search for any signs of Thrasher's presence. I only see the Barrier Brothers, the Russian Elites, Fishbowl Shawn, Eleven, Siv, and Gray. Thrasher's the only one missing. The other guys are going to have to hear about this. Unfortunately, coach probably took away their phones as well.

"Today," Coach Hill says. "We have a very special game for you. Today's challenge is team versus team. In the canoe cross, you guys learned to work together and succeeded as a whole. Now, we must move forth and challenge your teamwork in a physical competition. You boys will be excited to hear that it takes place indoors which includes air conditioning." The guys clap and cheer in joy. The cafeteria has air conditioning, but it's not that strong in a giant cabin like that. "We will be heading over to the Grotto and into The Burg, our laser lag arena." Some of the guys start small talking. "But before we start, you boys will head over to Counselor Campbell's Training Center and go through individual interviews. He'll ask you a series of questions, and all you have to do is answer them. So, head on over there and form a line to get started."

We all hurry in line behind Team Ink who beat us to it. The rain continues to soak our shirts, turning the ice blue color on our Team Frost shirts into a Caribbean bay. I stand in the middle of the bunch while the other guys go through their interviews.

Eventually, Team Ink finishes their interviews. Our guys begin to go in, one-by-one, into the Training Office. Max is the first one to go, and Miles watches his brother as he passes the two Hunters in the cabin. Max sits in a chair in front of Counselor Campbell's desk. One of the Hunters closes the door.

"What do you think he's going to ask?" Barrett says.

"I'm not sure," says I. "I couldn't tell ya."

After some time passes, it's Barrett's turn to walk inside. Siv walks down the steps and meets with the other guys by the campfire. The Hunters close the doors behind Barrett. He sits at Counselor Campbell's desk.

"Hi, Barrett," Counselor Campbell says.

"Hi," Barrett says.

"I'm going to ask you a few simple questions, they shouldn't take too long, and then I'll send you off."

"Okay."

"What position do you normally play?"

"Right wing."

Counselor Campbell writes his answer on a sheet of paper clipped to a clipboard. "What would you say is your top skill?"

"Um, I'd have to say my speed."

"Speedster. Gotchya." He makes note of that. "What's your biggest fear?"

"Heights."

"I don't blame ya for that one." He chuckles with Barrett. "And those are all the questions I have for ya."

"Really?"

"Yep. That's all I need from you."

"Sweet."

The Hunters open the door. Barrett strolls down the stairs. "Easy," he says to me. He works his way to the campfires.

I turn around and find Orson in another shivering stage. The Hunters wait for me to make my way up the steps. "Orson. Do you wanna go in front of me? I'll be right behind ya then." It takes him a while to make a choice, but I give him a little nudge. He accepts.

He walks up the steps and enters the room.

"Thought you weren't nervous?" Ash says.

He stands behind me in line, and Gray's behind him, the last one in line. "I'm not. Just trying to make Orson feel better."

"Yeah, okay."

"What's your problem, Ash?"

"Nothing."

"You seem salty at me again."

"What? What do you mean again?"

"Never mind."

"No. I want to hear this. What do you mean?"

"You know what I mean."

"I'm sorry, but I actually don't."

"Guys," Gray says. "Break it."

"Whatever," Ash says.

The door pops open. Orson moves down the steps.

"Good, Orson?" says I. He nods.

The Hunters stare at me with the door wide open. I march my way up the wet steps as the rain splashes off the wood. I walk to the top and pass the Hunters. The light flushes out as the door closes. Counselor Campbell puts a fresh sheet of paper on his clipboard. There're all sorts of black text on it like it's a school worksheet, blank lines needing to be filled out.

"Liam," Counselor Campbell says.

"Counselor," says I.

"I'm going to ask a few questions, then you can be on your way."

"Sounds easy enough."

"What position do you normally play?"

"Left wing." He writes it down.

"What's your strongest skill?"

"Strength."

"Strong." He notes it on the sheet.

"Me and Ash were actually called The Beasts since we had all the muscle on the team."

"Aw. So, you two played together?"

"Yeah. We played together in high school."

"Awesome. One more question before you go. What's your worst fear?"

"Worst fear . . . I don't know if I have one."

"What do you mean you don't have one?"

"I don't know what I'm afraid of."

"Are you afraid of spiders, heights, snakes, tight spaces, the vastness of space?"

"Not that I know of."

"Huh." He scribbles something down on the sheet. "Alright. You're all set."

The Hunters open the door. I make my way to the campfires. Ash heads inside for his interview, and Gray will finish it off last.

I find a seat next to Fishbowl Shawn and Eleven.

"Hey," Shawn says.

"Hey," says I. "How'd your guys' interview go?"

"It went fine," Eleven says. "Three quick questions."

"Same here," says I.

"They asked me what position I played, strongest skill, and worst fear," Eleven says.

"Same," Shawn says.

"What are your guys' biggest fear?" says I.

"Needles," Eleven says.

"Spiders," Shawn says. "What did you say, Liam?"

"I said snakes," says I. I just came up with something at the top of my head for them. I don't want the boys to see me as the weird kid without a fear.

"Oh yeah. Gross. Fuck nature." I'm offended by Shawn's comment. Nature's a God. I'd do anything to be out in the woods more often. That reminds me, I should take Barrett out on that hike that I promised we'd go on.

"So," says I. "Do you guys know what the others answered with?"

"Not sure," Eleven says. "All I know are some of their strengths."

"Like what?" says I.

"Well," Eleven continues, "Eli and Viktor, they're the Russian Elites. They're fricken smart, like, they're honestly geniuses in math and science. Then, Max and Miles, being twins and all, they were both D1 commits."

"What are they doing here then? Shouldn't they be training somewhere else?"

"I don't know, but I'm guessing they thought what we thought. This was a new and exciting opportunity that we were selected for." Eleven points over to Siv. "Now, Siv on the other hand, I don't know what his skill is, but I'm guessing he's just like any other goalie."

Coach Hill blows his whistle with rainwater spraying out of it. Dr. Fallenhein stands next to him. "Everyone's back from their individual meetings. It's time for the team versus team challenge. Follow me."

We follow coach to the Grotto and walk up the rocky staircase. We pass by the podium where Commander Moriz gave her speech. Moving forth, Coach Hill takes us into the cave. A huge metal door with the latch of an industrial freezer stands tall on the left.

Coach Hill pulls the handle back. "Boys, welcome to The Burg." He props the door open as a cold fog lingers from the darkness.

LASER LAG

Blacklights illuminate the room as the neon colors explode from the black walls. The air's thick, and the fog blurrifies the space around me. It's best that we're out of the downpouring rain now, but it's fricken freezing in here. Did the camp not know how to spell "Burg" correctly? It should be spelt Berg since it's cold like a mountain's peak, but it isn't. Blue and red lights glow from vests that align the wall on hangers. The lights reflect off the wall like a peaceful lake mirroring the moon. On the far wall, red vests hang to the right of a door, and the blue vests hang on the left. Coach Hill blocks the mystery door in between the vests. Dr. Fallenhein stands behind us. Team Ink groups over by the red vests; their coach speaks to them about the vests or something.

"Team Frost," Coach Hill says. "Welcome to your team versus team challenge. Today, you'll be competing Team Ink in laser lag. You'll be putting your team skills you used yesterday to the test. This game is a team deathmatch. The first team to reach fifty points wins the challenge."

"What do the losers have to do?" Shawn says. Eleven high fives him.

"Losers won't get a meal tonight," Coach Hill says.

"Wait," says I. "What?"

"It shouldn't be a concern. Should it?"

"They have an extra guy on their team."

Barrett steps forward. "Actually, we have two guys less than them now."

"I think it's completely acceptable," Coach Hill says.

"And why's that?" Gray asks. He never takes his backwards cap off.

"You have extra targets to shoot at."

Me and Barrett meet eyes wanting to roll them, but we know we shouldn't complain. A player complaining about something is the last thing a coach wants to deal with. You'll definitely be sat during a game if you do complain. All though, if we can get the whole team to complain about it at once, then we can start a revolution and overthrow the dictator. Not such a bad idea, but a couple of players won't be a downfall for us. I hope.

"Team Ink is red team," Coach Hill says. "You guys will be blue. You'll throw these vests over your head like your shoulder pads for hockey, then you'll strap them in on the sides with the buckles. Your guns are attached to the vest. It'll shoot a laser beam with a pull of the trigger, but they'll only work when the match starts. Your guys' deployment will be in the front left corner when you walk in. Team Ink's deployment will be in the far back on the right. These deployments will be your reloading stations after you get shot. You must help your wounded teammates back to deployment in order to save them. Every wounded player has thirty seconds to make it back or else they're eliminated from the match. With me so far?" We nod. "When you divide the map in half, your side on the left is winter themed for Team Frost. On the right half with Team Ink is the hot zone. I'd recommend thinking things out before running around the map. There are three lanes you can head down. You'll see your lanes consist of a ruined medieval castle, an icehouse which sits in the center lane, and an igloo right in front of your deployment." Coach Hill glances back to Dr. Fallenhein. He's still wearing his black lab coat and funky glowing glasses. "Is that all, Dr. Fallenhein?"

"I believe so," he says. "Let's go glow em up."

"Alright, boys. Suit up."

We dart to the blue glowing vests. I grab a vest from its hook, and it's cool to the touch. When I throw the bulky vest on, it makes me feel like I'm in outer space floating in liquid nitrogen. The plastic lights on my shoulder blind me while I search for the dangling buckles. I feel the metal clips then hook them together out front. On my side, Barrett clips the back clips on his vests.

"Yo," says I. "Barrett."

"Yeah?" he says.

"Can you clip my back ones for me?"

"Sure."

"Thank you."

Barrett buckles the clips. "There ya go."

"You're the best."

My gun dangles off to the side and clangs against my leg. I pull on the tube of the gun, then I grab its handle. The gun appears to be a mock of the TAR-21; it has a grip out in front with a longer mag clip in the back. It has nice shoulder support, and it'll be nice for range, at least in laser lag.

On the other side of the room, Team Ink is suited and ready. Their coaches lead the way to the door. The head coach pushes Coach Hill out of the way as he opens the door to The Burg. Coach Hill glares at him while the head coach smiles back.

"Coach Lac," Coach Hill says. "You think you're so tough."

"I don't think I'm tough," he says. "I know I'm tough."

"Big words for a small guy." Coach Hill got him there. Lac's like the height of The Dragon's coach back in high school. Oh my God. Did I just say that? Man, I feel old already.

"I'll get the tissue box ready for you."

"Save it for yourself." Coach turns around. Team Ink finishes entering The Burg. "You guys ready?"

We bounce off the ground like rabbits and scream for Team Ink's defeat. Ash and Louie raise their guns in the air and lead our team through the door and into The Burg.

Now I know why they call it The Burg. It's a fricken fortress.

We walk inside the cockpit of a plane wreck. Hard EDM music blasts through speakers which vibrates the floor. I follow the guys as we walk through the plane which has seats on the left side, right side, and middle. Some of the seats are missing, probably so no one can just lay down on the floor and hide the whole game. In the back, a few walls divide space from the airplane seats. Behind the wall is a hallway that connects our winter theme to Team Ink's hot zone. I turn around and find the upper-class floor of the plane exposed like a sniper's nest. That's gotta be a sniping trap. Two twisting staircases lead up to it on each side.

When we turn left at the back of the plane, we find a ruined-stone wall in our way. We turn right. Behind the small plane wreck simulation, there are stairs climbing to an upper platform. Ash decides to break off and run-up to the top of it.

"It's another lane," Ash says. "The stairs just go back down to their side." He runs back down the stairs. Louie and Ash continue into the stone building. It's the ruined castle. It's almost pitch-black here. A wall divides the whole lane from the rest of the map. The walls form a few sniping windows, creating a weird S-shape to scurry through. From the viewing window in the back, there's a nice vantage point to camp and shoot the guys coming up the staircase.

At the end of the ruined castle is the corner of the map, but it's not our corner deployment. Ash and Louie take a sharp left and follow the back wall. Cold blue lights that mimic the cold fade in as we look through the middle lane of the map. More fog swirls in front of us, even more than the scent of those cinnamon rolls Dr. Fallenhein gave to us this morning. Through the two open doorways that look like the double set of french doors in The Barn is the icehouse. The icehouse contains two windows that look into the wrecked plane's windows.

In the final lane is the igloo, and the igloo is right in front of our blue deployment base. The deployment sits in the corner in front of us, protected by towering walls.

We all huddle into a waddle in the corner, and I'm in the middle of everyone. A large screen glows on the wall to my left. It has our names on it and a scoreboard for both teams. Suddenly, the blue lights strobe, then they steady back to their normal, settled glow.

"Quiet guys," Louie says. "Go ahead, Ash."

Ash yells over the loud EDM music, "We need a plan!"

"What kind of plan?" Gray says.

"We need to split up and have designated lanes."

"How should we do that?" Siv says.

"Viktor and I have an idea," Eli says.

"Spill it," Ash says.

"Since Max and Miles play defense, they should camp in the icehouse and protect our base. Me and Viktor will win control of the upper deck in the plane wreck."

"What happens if you guys are trapped up there and we can't save you?" says I.

"We're smart," Viktor says. "Don't worry about us."

"Yeah," Shawn says. "They're the Russian Elites."

"Continue, Eli," Louie says.

"Okay," he says. "So, there are nine of you left. We should have four guys in the igloo lane to the right here, and then four in the ruined castle on the far left."

"How bout the last guy?" Ash says.

"I think we should have a guy saving the wounded, if they need it that is."

"Orson can do that," Ash says.

"No," says I. "We can't leave him alone."

"He'll be fine," Ash says.

"No. He's coming with me."

"I can do it," Eleven says. "I'll be the menace-medic."

"Alright," Viktor says. "Four will go to the ruined castle, and four will enter the igloo."

The EDM music softens. A deep, dark voice floats in the fog. "The match will begin in ten seconds." We all start to prepare for our moves. I can't tell which direction I'm heading; it's either the igloo, or the ruined castle. Wish they would have clarified the groups of four. Sweat builds under my hand from the gun. The weapon shakes and rattles as a blue light glows inside a circular bubble above the ammunition clip. The blue light fills the bubble like rushing water, then it drains down a line which leads to the end of the barrel. The lights strobe again, flexing the air faster and faster as a storm has approached. Team Ink turns into a bunch of gorillas, screaming their voices into the air. "Three." Here we go. "Two." A meal is on the line for this. "One." The lights flicker into seizures as the EDM music builds into a deep bass drop. "Tag the enemies."

The Russian Elites hurry around the wall and through the igloo. They scurry over to their spot in the upper-class deck of the plane wreck. Ash, Louie, backwards cap Gray, and fishbowl Shawn rush into the igloo. I twist around and see the Barrier

Brothers moving to their icehouse to camp out. Eleven stays put by the scoreboard and watches it. Siv and Barrett sneak over to the ruined castle with their guns ready to fire. Orson stands beside me.

"Let's follow them," says I.

Me and Orson catch up with them, finding the lane of the ruined castle.

"I'll take the back window here and watch the staircase," Barrett says. "Siv, take the wall in front of me on the left there."

"Wait," Siv says. "Which one?"

"The L-shaped one on the wall there."

"Oh, okay." He scurries over to his spot and kneels down behind the broken wall.

"What should we do?" says I.

"Go through and enter the plane wreck," Barrett says. "Find a spot in there to camp."

"Wait." I pull Barrett to the side. "Orson should stay back."

"You think?"

"I know he wants to."

Barrett judges Orson. Orson watches the staircase with the eyes of an owl. "Okay."

I walk to Orson. "Hey. You'll camp here behind this window. You'll be safer here."

"You shoot anyone who heads over that staircase, okay?" Barrett says.

"Okay," Orson says.

"Alright," says I. "Let's go turn them into sieves."

"Hey," Siv says. "We don't all have holes in us." A laser

blasts by Siv's head. He jolts around and finds two red players at the top of the staircase. "Shoot, Orson!"

Me and Barrett duck behind Orson's wall. While they shoot at the red guys, I crouch behind Siv, then I roll over to the dividing wall and hide from the staircase shooters. Barrett hurries over in an immense laser storm. Blue and red lasers fly everywhere like shooting stars. I peek around the wall and find the outside foundation of the plane wreck, but there's a good amount of exposure from the stairs.

One of the red guys steps all the way to the top of the platform and exposes himself. He sprays his gun at Siv, but Siv fires back and hits him dead in the chest. The red lights on the guy blink as he falls and rolls backwards down their side of the steps. Me and Barrett quickly maneuver out from the ruined castle and flush tight against the plane's foundation. On my left, the Barrier Brothers shoot from the two windows of the icehouse, and on the far lane, Shawn camps in a window of the igloo, aiming in our direction.

I peek my head around the corner, catching a glimpse in the open hall of the wrecked airplane. I can't see anyone camping on the floor in the airplane seats. Peeking even further down the hall, I spot a red light moving from behind the other doorway.

"Hold on," says I. "I see someone."

"Can you shoot him?" Barrett says.

I take a deep breath, then I jump through the doorway. A red guy runs inside the hall. I spray a few shots at his chest. He falls to the floor and screams. His body shakes like he's having a seizure from the strobe lights or something. I hide back behind the wall with Barrett while we listen to him scream for help. I peek around the wall and find another red guy running through. I move to the doorway and spray more shots at his chest. He too falls down to the floor and screams. Both guys lie on the floor, shaking. I return to Barrett along the wall.

"Something's not right," says I.

"What's happening?" Barrett says.

"I don't know. They just fall when you shoot them." Around the corner, Hunters intrude the plane wreck from the cockpit. They grasp onto the red guys' vests and drag them out. "The Hunters. They're dragging them out."

"What?"

"It's been thirty seconds. No one rescued them."

"They're eliminated now."

"Yeah. Even numbers now too."

"That's good, Liam. That's fricken good."

I move into the plane with Barrett and into the hall. I look around the backseat wall to discover Eli and Viktor on top of the upper deck. They fire their blue streaks in a red meteor shower.

"C'mon," says I. "Let's move down the hall."

Carefully, we cross from our backseat wall to the middle backseat wall in the hall. I peer around the middle wall and look through the destroyed line of airplane windows. I can see an abandoned jungle building in the far back corner where the Russian Elites shoot into. In the middle, there's a big bush with two windows, just like the icehouse.

"Imma cross over to the last wall here and look around the corner," says I.

"Okay," Barrett says. "I'll be right behind ya."

I crawl to the last backwall. When I examine the hot zone through the doorway, I find a dried-out sauna that's sunken into the ground and surrounded by bushes. You can only enter the sauna by the staircase lane or jumping over the bush. A red guy spots my shoulder's blue light from behind the sunken sauna. That's where their deployment is located. The red guy fires at me, but I back up in time and miss his spray fire. I peer at Barrett as a laser darts to his chest. The light blinks while he collapses to the floor. He screams my name. While he screams on the floor, I wait. From our side of the plane, I find Eleven sprinting behind the icehouse. Then, he squints down the hall and discovers Barrett.

The red guy fires away at Eleven, and he shoots right back at him. I duck and hurry over to Barrett. I help him onto his feet as Eleven distracts the red guy. I hustle Barrett out of the plane wreck. We move in between the icehouse and ruined castle to the back wall. I bring him to the deployment area where his vest lights up blue again. He stops screaming, but he whines on the floor.

"Barrett?" says I. He can't hear me over the music. "Barrett!" I kneel next to him. I pick his head up, pointing his focus to me. "Just breathe! Breathe, Barrett."

"It hurts," Barrett says. "It's a fricken taser."

"What?"

"It felt like an electrical shock from like a taser or something, but it was constant."

"Do you still feel it?"

"No, but it still burns. It was like a thousand needles poking into my muscles."

"Geezes. What kind of camp is this?"

"A fucking concentration camp. That's what it is."

"We need to tell the others. Go tell the Barrier Brothers, Siv, and Orson." I pull him up. We split ways.

I maneuver through the walls to the igloo. Ash and Gray camp by the door that directs to Viktor's and Eli's sniping nest. Shawn still camps in his little window. Through a window on the right side of Shawn is Louie; he crouches on the ground and shoots to the other side of the plane.

I tap Ash's shoulder. "Ash."

"What?"

"Come here." He hesitates to get up, but he sees the urgency in my eyes. "We need to get out of here."

"Um. Why?"

"These vests . . . Yeah, they put us in an electrical shock."

"You're serious?"

"Yes."

"Well, how bad does it hurt?"

"I don't know. Barrett was screaming his head off."

"I need to feel it for myself."

"What?"

"Shoot me."

"I'm not shooting you."

"Shoot me. I'll be fine."

"Is there friendly fire though?"

"Guess we'll find out."

I really don't want to shoot him, but I do as he wants. I pull the trigger as lasers spray into his chest light. He howls out a scream as he catches himself on the igloo's wall. He slides down to the floor in shock. I grasp onto his vest and pull him to deployment. The shock stops.

"Fuck!" he yells. "Why did you shoot me?"

"You told me to. You good?"

"This sucks."

The scoreboard says we're in the lead: 7-3. "Oh my God," says I. "We need to get to fifty fast."

"How? This is just a loop of torture."

"We need to push."

"You want us to run to their side? Coach told us not to."

"Coach said to be careful," says I. "But to be honest, I want to get out of here anyway I can."

"So, what's your plan with the push?" Ash asks.

"We wound as many as we can. Then, we push the surviving shooters into their deployment and trap them."

"Then what do we do? They're in their healing corner."

"Then the other wounded soldiers will be eliminated after thirty seconds."

"Yes. I like that. Or even better, we push them from their deployment corner, so they won't get to it."

"That'll be tricky, but let's do it."

"I'll talk to my guys. You let the others know."

"Meet back here."

Me and Ash part ways. I rush to Max and Miles and tell them the plan. They both agree to it, especially after the news of the electrical shock. I move to the castle ruins where Orson and Siv continue to fire away at a red guy hiding behind the staircase.

"Guys!" yells I.

"What is it!" Siv yells.

"Come to deployment."

"What?"

"Trust me. We have a battle plan, but we have to be fast."

"Geezes." Siv sprays away as he stands and treads backwards. Orson stays in the middle of us.

"What are we doing, Liam?" Barrett says.

"We're gonna push them," says I.

"I can't go back out there."

"We have to do this. The faster we do this, the quicker we can leave."

Gray, Louie, Shawn, and Ash group up with us in the back corner.

"Eli and Viktor are making their way back," Ash says.

"We need to do this now," says I.

"Dude," Siv says. "They've caught on early."

Max and Miles spin around where two red guys pop out from the ruined castle. The Barrier Brothers are both shot down into their screaming pains. Siv and Louie paint their lasers all over the two guys. They collapse. I crawl under the bullets of color and pull the brothers behind the deployment wall.

"Stay in the walls," says I. "Shoot as many guys as you can. You'll be safe in deployment."

"What are you saying?" Gray says. I'm still surprised he has his cap on.

"We're going to lure them in."

Viktor and Eli backpedal from the igloo and into deployment. "Guys," Viktor says. "They're all coming for us."

"Just keep shooting at them!" yells I. "Just stay behind deployment."

The two red guys on the ground by the castle lose their lights. Twelve guys left.

Sighting through the doorway of the igloo, The Russian Elites shoot at a red guy sprinting through the wrecked plane's windows. Eli fires at his shoulder, dropping him like an anchor. Another red guy pops out in the igloo's doorway and shoots head-on. He's hitting Viktor's chest pad, but he's in no pain. Viktor sends his blue lasers to him and collapses another player. Ten reds left.

Two Team Ink players pop out from the wall with the two french doorways. I spray my gun at the far guy while Louie shoots down the one in front. Eight players left.

Eli and Viktor spot a red guy pulling out the wounded soldier from inside the airplane. They spray him down. Seven Players left.

"We need to push, now," Eli says.

"Copy that," Louie says.

"Let's break into our squads," Ash says. "Russian Elites and Barrier Brothers join together. You guys will take middle lane. My squad has right. Liam, yours has left."

We break into our three lanes again. Me, Barrett, Siv, and Orson tiptoe through the ruined castle. I keep my gun pointed in front me as I jolt around the corner walls. No one sits behind the window wall, and no one crouches behind the L-shaped wall.

"Staircase?" says I.

"Clear," Barrett says.

I point my gun around the corner to the siding of the wrecked airplane. Suddenly, a red guy slides out from behind the ruined castle wall and grips onto my gun. Barrett steps out and aims for his shoulder. He fires away and strikes his red light. The guy fumbles onto the ground into his shaking seizure. Six guys left.

"Nice shot, Barrett," says I.

Now, we make our way up the staircase.

In the middle lane, the Russian Elites and Barrier Brothers enter the plane from both sides; the back wall and cockpit area. Two red guys pop up in the broken windows. The boys flare their lasers and shoot the red guys down. Four guys left.

Ash, Louie, Gray, and Shawn sneak upon the upper-class deck and move down the spiral steps to the abandoned jungle building. As Ash leads them in, a guy fires at his head from behind a broken wall. Ash shoots him dead on in the chest. He moves his line forward through the building. A window stands in front of him. He looks through the window and sees a red guy hiding in a crouch. He takes his gun, touches the barrel to his shoulder light, and executes him. Two guys left.

As I walk down the steps, a guy rampages us in shots from the dried-up sauna. I spray fire to distract the guy on me as Barrett moves down the steps. Siv joins in with me, not because he has to, but because he wants to. Barrett reaches the bottom step and moves around the sauna wall. He shoots the red guy down.

We all converge at the back wall in the hot zone. "Is that all of them?" Gray says.

I discover Team Ink's scoreboard in the back corner. One guy's left. It's Ben. "There's one more," says I.

When I hustle back to my group, I catch a red light running through the windows of the wrecked airplane. I make my way over to the plane, passing the giant bush. "Liam?" Louie says.

I tiptoe to the front entrance of the airplane. The EDM music continues to blare inside The Burg. I make it to the doorway, then peek to the left corner. Nothing. I tiptoe a few more steps. I turn the corner, entering the middle aisle of seats. No one's lying on the floor. A gun yanks my neck back as Ben stands behind me in a chokehold.

"Charge!" Orson yells.

"Charge!" the boys holler back. They charge at Ben as he releases me. I spin around while he sends a laser through my chest pad. An electrical charge tightens my muscles like a vacuum imploding my body. A million stingers dig down into my skin. Heat burns through the skin as my blood boils in my veins. Orson shoots Ben in the shoulders. He collapses. The guys pick me up and take me to our deployment, saving me in time before my thirty seconds are up.

Our plan worked. We succeed as a team and receive a meal after all.

SUMMER BLIZZARD

We follow Coach Hill out of the Grotto and into the wet grass. The rain has stopped, but the clouds still linger. He takes us into the cafeteria for our awarding meal. Pizzas line up on the food shelf, topped with fresh cheese and greasy pepperoni. Gray leads us to the trays and starts digging in. While I wait in line, I find Commander Moriz strolling inside. Her heels click against the floor as her yellow dress swifts like a butterflies' wings. Coach Hill approaches her, then shakes her hand. Dr. Fallenhein joins the party, walking inside with the same lab coat as usual. While I watch them talk, I find Ash standing behind me.

"Smells like Carbone's," says I.

"Yep," Ash says.

"Alright, man. What's up?"

"Nothing."

"Come on. It doesn't take a skip of a rock to see something's rippling inside of you." He crosses his arms. "Ash."

"Fuck off, Liam."

Louie overhears our conversation. I jolt around and move forward. A fire erupts in my throat, thinning my appetite for food. Ash keeps pushing me away from shore and out into open water. I'm losing him, but he isn't telling me why, and I can't figure out what's up with him. Ever since Thrasher was taken away, he's been salty towards me. It's just like the time at Carbone's.

I grab a few slices of pepperoni pizza and find a seat near Barrett out front. Orson sits on the other side of Barrett, and Max and Miles take a seat in front of us. Ash's breeze brushes against my shirt as he sails down the aisle to the end table. Him and Louie eat with the Russian Elites and backwards hat Gray. Siv joins us. Fishbowl Shawn and Eleven join the other group. While Ash devours his food like a vicious bear, I glance outside the cafeteria windows. Team Ink makes their way to the cabins, Ben being one of the guys in front of the bulk.

"I feel bad," says I.

Barrett turns his eyes to the rest of our team. "Them?"

"No. Team Ink. They don't get a meal tonight."

"I'd have to agree."

"Our father would kill us if he knew we didn't eat a healthy meal," Miles says. His cross-necklace dangles over his pizza, licking the grease right off its cheesy surface.

"Do you have strict parents?" says I.

"No," Miles says. "Not strict."

"Our father's a dictator," Max says. "He forced us to play hockey. I don't regret him for doing so, but he pressures us. He pressures us too much."

"He starves us on game days," Miles says. "He doesn't let us hang out with our friends. He signs us up for these intense camps where the coaches abuse us."

"He wants us to be big in the hockey world. Well, not big. Huge."

"Look where you are though," Barrett says. "I'm sure you've been through a lot, but you're literally D1 commits who've been selected at Camp Kelmo."

"Well, I don't know if that's an accomplishment," says I. "Guys, what kind of camp is this? I didn't think these tests were going to be fatal."

"Fatal?" Miles says.

"Orson could have drowned out there on the lake. Then, when I didn't think things could get worse, people were being electrocuted in laser tag."

"I don't know," says Max. "I can't seem to tell the difference with camps anymore. It's just pain and pain and more pain. I wish mom was still with us."

"You lost your mom?" says I.

"Well," Miles says. "She divorced our father, but she was too scared to take us with her."

"She abandoned us," Max says.

"She still loves us."

"How do you know that?"

"I just do. I bet she thinks about us every day."

"Then why hasn't she come back for us?

"She will."

"It's been thirteen years, Miles." They both turn their faces to their trays. The twin brothers do have identical feelings.

"In the meantime, I don't want to see my parents again," Barrett says. Max and Miles jump their eyes to him in sync. "I don't think I can handle it anymore. All they do is argue. They argue and cry and all I can do is listen to them." I set my hand on Barrett's shoulder. "We're homeless."

My vision fades out into black ice. The photo of me and my father back home in my bedroom melts in my mind. We were in The Barn for our team's photoshoot my Bantam year. We took a portrait together. He wore his coaching helmet and held his hockey stick like a giant candy cane, and I stood next to him with my arm wrapped around him. Bantams may have been the best years of my hockey career. I really wish I could say high school topped them all, but that topping melted to the bottom of the bowl.

"Are you okay, Liam?" Barrett says.

"Yeah," says I. "I'm fine."

I discover my eyes googling in water. Max and Miles see it too, but they pretend like they don't and distract themselves. The clicking of heels draws our attention to Commander Moriz who marches in front of the pizza shelves. She faces us in a sharp posture. Coach Hill and Dr. Fallenhein stand to the side and observe.

"Congratulations," Commander Moriz says. "It seems that Team Frost knew what they were doing in The Burg. You guys have been doing remarkable teamwork. As you can see, teamwork brings you rewards in the end. Winning a tournament isn't about scoring goals or being the strongest out of all teams, but it's about the chemistry you have with one another. You guys have one final test tomorrow before we hop on the ice. Tomorrow is the individual agility challenge which will focus on your strength and speed. Since you guys won today, you'll be the first ones to get it over with tomorrow, Team Ink will finish last. Make sure you get some good muscle stretches in. You'll need it." Louie throws his hand into the air. "Question?"

"Yeah," he says. "Where's our friend, Thrasher?"

"Thrasher went home unfortunately." Louie lowers his hand. Orson's lips tremble. "Don't worry about the fairness of teams. Team Ink has two goalies, which helps even everything out."

"How so?" says I. "We were one short, then two short."

"Quantity doesn't matter, sweetie. Quality does."

"Three guys targeted my friend. He couldn't do anything. All he could do was take the pain. Later that night, he committed suicide."

Commander Moriz clicks her heels over to me. She squats next to me, face to face. "What's your name, sweetie?"

"Liam."

"Awe. Liam. I remember you."

"What do you mean?"

"You're the boy who didn't list a fear in Counselor Campbell's interview."

"I'm not afraid of anything."

"Oh, sweetie. Everybody's afraid of something." She lifts

onto her feet again and scans the table. "I'll see you all tomorrow after your training is complete."

Barrett taps my shoulder. "You didn't tell them your fear?"

"I don't have one."

"Spiders? Heights? Claustrophobia?"

"Not that I know of. I don't know what my fear is. I don't know if I have one."

"Strong dude."

Coach Hill walks to the front. "Finish your meal, boys. We'll be out of here in five."

My pizza erodes upon my tray. It's probably cold now since I haven't taken a bite out of it. Even though it's summer with the heat blazing the bees, there's an arctic wave crashing over me. It feels just as cold as my senior year in high school. That year brings blizzards back into my mind, chilling me down to the bone.

I don't know where Thrasher is at this point, but I also don't know why Ash hibernates from me. Barrett is all I got right now. That reminds me, I should probably go on that hike that I promised him.

TIPSY TREETOPS

The night burns away in the morning light. The birds are back outside tweeting their songs as the rain has passed. Water blankets the shoreline in calming waves. A puddle reflects the greenery from the nearby hill, that is until Eleven kicks the water at Shawn's legs. Muddy water drips down the back of Shawn's leg and dissolves into his sock. Shawn finds a smaller puddle and kicks the water back at Eleven. Their legs look like chocolate covered cannolis.

Coach Hill and Dr. Fallenhein are taking us through the woods to our final test. Today deals with individual agility. I don't know how Orson's going to do alone. After everything we've been through so far, I can't expect him to be comfortable with any of this. The other guys seem to be doing fine. Ash's friends want more action. They're a bunch of adrenaline junkies wanting to jump off a cliff's edge to find out if they can fly.

Coach Hill stops. He turns around and places his fists on his waist. "Welcome to the treetops course." Over Coach Hill's head is a wooden course in the lush trees. A butterfly flies out in front of my eyes and tours me through the whole course. There's a bouncy bridge, monkey bars, and a pole that acts like a tight rope. At the end, a zipline rips through the trees and over the path we entered on. Team Ink walks beneath it and meets behind our group with their coaches. Ben's out front again, chit chatting with his friends. I turn so he doesn't find me staring at him again.

"Dude," Gray says. "This looks epic."

"Haven't been on a treetops course since middle school," says I.

"Are they hard?"

"Depends if you're in shape or not, and your balance needs to be spot on."

"What if you fall?"

"There are harnesses that'll keep you safe. If you fall, you just dangle there like wind chimes, but you need abs to get yourself back on course."

"Oh. I got abs. Piece of cake." Okay, Mr. Cocky. I do wish I had his abs though.

"Alright, boys," Coach Hill says. "Your final test is an individual agility challenge. You must make it across the bridge, the monkey bars, and the tight pipe. At the end, you'll get to sit on the zipline ride and coast your way back."

Dr. Fallenhein moves forth. "Since you guys won laser lag, Commander Moriz rewards you with going first." He scans the names on his clipboard. "First up. Barrett."

I search for Barrett in the thicket of our team. The boys spread out like he's a repulsive magnet. Barrett's teeth clatter together like a skeleton decoration. The rest of my team just stares at him while he stands there in shock.

"Come on, Barrett," Coach Hill says. "Burning daylight here."

I push through Siv and Orson and walk in front of Barrett. "Barrett. Talk to me." Dr. Fallenhein slaps his clipboard against his leg.

"I can't do it," Barrett says.

"Of course, you can. You're strong, Barrett."

"What if I fall?"

"You'll be just fine. There's a harness and everything that'll keep you safe." I spin to the coaches. They stare at us. I inspect the course for the ziplines to connect the harnesses to, but there's nothing hanging above the course, not even handrails. "Where are the harnesses?"

"There aren't any," Coach Hill says.

"No," says I. "We're not doing this course."

"You'll do what you are told to do."

"Can't you see that someone's going to get hurt?"

"It's not that high off the ground."

"There's a steep hill sloping down from under the course."

"Here's the thing boys. If you're a leader, a true leader, a strong leader, you would fight anything that threatens you." Coach Hill scans Dr. Fallenhein's clipboard. "Scratch Barrett for now." He points at me. "Liam. You're up."

It's not worth the challenge. A person with strength would walk away from this. Someone's going to hurt themselves up there. This camp kills. I wrap my arm around Barrett's shoulder and steal him from the crowd. We make our way around Team Ink as Ben and his teammates stare.

"What?" Ben says. "Too weak to handle the ropes?" I ignore him. "So, you're just not gonna talk like always."

Just ignore him, Liam. A shock drops me to my knees. My elbows and face slam into the mucky mud. The blood in my veins crawls its way back into my muscles, gaining the strength back that I lost. Team Ink turns into hyenas. I get off the muddy ground and find myself being laughed at, even by Ash. Besides Ash, Dr. Fallenhein holds a laser pointer. He holds it in his hand, ready to fire another laser at me.

"Liam," Coach Hill says. "You'll do as we say. Complete this challenge, then you won't have a problem. If you try to run, Dr. Fallenhein will have to zap you again. You may even have to be benched. I don't think you want to be a benchwarmer. Do ya?"

Barrett backs into our group again while keeping his eyes on me. I take my muddy face through the boys and limp to the ladder of the ropes course.

Viktor leans into Eli, "I knew those cinnamon rolls had a hint of something."

"Yeah," Eli says. "Some sort of chemical."

"A metal perhaps."

The ladder dangles from the first platform. It sits inside of a V in the tree's base. I grab one of the wooden steps and start my climb. My hands are wet with sweat, making them slick on my grips. Below, the ladder twists around my feet, wanting to tangle them in a bunch of vines. I pause for a few seconds for the ladder to steady itself, then I continue to climb. I find the top platform. I push my hands on the platform's floor and stretch my legs to the top. While I stand, I discover a splinter stuck in my finger. I try to pinch it out, but it stabs back like the needle in the haystack.

The first obstacle awaits. It's the bouncy bridge. There're no rails on the sides, just some wooden planks to hop across. Fifteen planks lead me to the other platform, and that's where the forest drops off. A group of gnats swarms around my head. I swat at them. Then, an itch darts in my right leg. I discover a mosquito sucking the blood out of me. I smack it, splattering the blood on my sweaty hand.

"Let's go, Liam," Gray chants. "You got this." Some of the other boys cheer with him.

I hover my first step over the wooden plank. I push upon it to find the bouncy bridge pretty sturdy. It doesn't seem to twist a lot, but it'll for sure be bouncy in the middle. I blast my back foot to the second plank. My arms span apart from each other like the wings on an airplane. I take my third step, then my fourth, then my fifth. Just don't look down. Keep your focus on the platform in front of you. Feel the steps, feel the gaps, and feel the air. Suddenly, I feel my body tilting to the right. I angle my wings to the left and bend my knees to gain my balance again. My legs shake as the bridge begins to vibrate with them. Take a deep breath. You're almost through, Liam. I make my seventh step, then my eighth, then my ninth. I sprint the remaining steps. I trip over the edge of the platform and crash upon it. In front of me, under the platform, I see the tops of the trees across a dense forest. The hill drops here, I just hope that I won't drop.

The second obstacle is the monkey bars. I wipe the blood and sweat on my shorts. The monkey bars aren't something from a playground though. They're dangling ropes with lips at the end of them. I grip my hands on the first two ropes. I drop my feet from the platform as they dangle above the steep downhill. I swing my left hand to the next rope, then my right. Butterflies flutter in my stomach, and my feet tingle like the fizz in lemon-lime pop. The ropes grease my hands in sweat. Just book it, Liam. Get it done and over with. I turn on my monkey skills and cross the ropes in a blazing wildfire. Before I know it, I'm crashing down on the other platform. My hands burn from the grainy ropes, and my arms tighten into boa constrictors. The boys continue to cheer me on. Coach Hill watches Dr. Fallenhein make notes on his clipboard.

The last obstacle. It's a skinny metal pole, mimicking a tight rope. I take a few deep breaths before I span into an airplane again. I place my left foot on the pole. Knowing I can't do this without looking down, I watch my feet and focus on only my feet. Everything under my feet and the pole blurrifies. My foot steps off the platform and in front of my other foot. While I walk across, I tilt from left to right, keeping my balance steady. A gusty breeze blows over the treetops. I freeze and balance out the wind as it wants to push me off. The muscles in my legs contract. Keep going and get this over with. The end is in front of you. I move again, crossing my legs over and over again like overspeed; just cross your legs over each other while you skate and you'll get that rocket speed. Another swarm of gnats flies around my head. While I walk through them, one ends up in my throat. My foot slips to the side of the pole. I fall forward and wrap my arms around the pole. My body spins under the pole as I turn into a sloth, dangling from its branch. I continue my way down the pole, scooting my arms and legs to the platform. With a weird twist of my chest, I reach an arm out for the platform. I release a foot from the pole and launch my other hand onto the platform. I pull my body up and rest on the structure, regaining my breath.

The boys give a round of applause. While my body shakes in pain, I wipe the sweat off my forehead and bow to the crowd. Behind me, the lounge of the zipline awaits. I sink down into the seat. A cord hangs above me off to the side. I place my hand on its handle and view my path through the trees. With a yank of the cord, my seat releases and flings down the zipline. I grasp onto the seat as the wind pushes me back. I find myself giggling on the zipline. My feet brush green plants while zipping by. A huge tree towers in front of me, and I'm heading right for it. I lose my smile, and I scream inside my head. My hands raise out in front of me, and my eyes flush shut. My body jolts forward in a choke.

The brake rebounds me away from the tree. When the seat comes to a complete stop, I hop off. Coach Hill points to the seat. "Pull the handle again." I pull the handle from before, the seat rolls back up the zipline by itself. Shawn and Eleven wave me down. I hustle over to them and join my teammates.

"That was dope," Eleven says.

"Thanks, Eleven," says I. "Almost died there."

"That was so sick though," Shawn says. "You were hanging from the fricken pole."

Behind Shawn and Eleven, Orson stares at me. I stroll to him.

"Orson," says I. "Do you think you can make it?" He bounces his eyes to the mud.

Gasps radiate through the groups. I jolt my eyes to find a body falling from the monkey bars and behind the steep hill. My hand launches up to my mouth. Ash, Louie, and the Barrier Brothers run over to the fallen soldier. I search around my group to see who's missing.

"Orson," says I. "Where's Barrett?" Ash and Louie carry a moaning boy up the steep hill. It's Barrett. "Oh my God." I rush to Barrett. "Barrett! Are you okay?"

"I feel . . . dizzy," he says.

"Give him to me." Ash and Louie move one of his arms around my neck. I walk him over to Coach Hill and Dr. Fallenhein. "I'm taking him back to the cabin."

"Put him in the cabin," Coach Hill says. "But then the rest of us meet at the Grotto. Commander Moriz has a speech to commence."

Me and Barrett push past the teams and through the woods. Eventually, we make it back. Counselor Campbell notices Barrett limping as I help him to Cabin 5.

"Woah," Counselor Campbell says. "What the hell happened to him?"

"He fell in training. He fell in the treetops course you devils designed." I march Barrett over to the back bunk, sliding him into Louie's bed. Counselor Campbell follows us inside. "Get some rest, Barrett. I'll get you some water."

"How did he fall?" Counselor Campbell says.

"Don't act like you don't fucking know."

He asks Barrett, "Well weren't you wearing a harness?"

"There weren't any harnesses," says I. I grab Barrett's water bottle from his hockey bag and fill it with sink water.

"I never thought anyone would get hurt. I mean, I knew the camp was going to be challenging and over the top, but no one's supposed to get hurt."

"That's all that's been happening. My friend almost died because he can't swim. We were fricken electrocuted in laser lag. And now my friend fell off the treetops with no safety net." The water floods out from the bottle. I twist the faucet off and put the cover on. I walk it over to Barrett's side on the floor, then I sit beside him on the bed. The back of my hand caresses his forehead. "How are ya feeling?"

"Something's banging inside of my head," Barrett says.

I turn to Counselor Campbell. "He should see a doctor. He probably has a concussion."

"Dr. Fallenhein could probably check him out."

"No. He needs to go home."

"You can't go home."

"What?"

"Commander Moriz doesn't want anyone leaving camp. It's

131

what you guys signed up for. You were selected to serve at this special camp, and now you must finish your duty here."

"This place isn't a hockey camp. It's a fucking prison."

I roll to my side next to Barrett and turn away from Counselor Campbell. I can hear him crouching next to me.

"How badly do you want to get out of here?" Counselor Campbell says. Twisting to him, he discovers the stream of tears flowing down my face. "Alright, Liam. I'll tell you what. I'll help you get out of here, but we can't talk here. We'll have to talk in my office."

"Coach Hill's enforcing us to meet outside of the Grotto for Commander Moriz."

"Shit. Okay. I'll figure out a time to meet with you. Just keep your head down and do what they tell you."

Counselor Campbell exits the cabin. Before I leave Barrett in the cabin alone, I lock my arms around him for a gentle hug. It's time to march back to the Grotto.

MOONLIGHT

Green vines and lush leaves swing over the Grotto. The podium awaits for Commander Moriz's arrival. Team Ink finishes their last guys over at the treetops, some of them scarred and muddy, but most guys made it through. I wouldn't doubt if some of them crawled their way across the bouncy bridge and pole. Their hands burn in scars and blisters. On our team, Siv appears to be the only one muddy. Everyone else seems clean, sweaty as heck though. The humidity hasn't left, leaving us inside of a jungle.

Team Ink acts like there's an invisible wall that divides us. There's just the slightest gap between our teams, and they won't melt together. Ben's clothes are lean and clean. I wonder if he kissed his way out of it. I actually thought we were getting somewhere in life. I thought we were uniting as friends that senior year. He gave me the C from his jersey, he started to look up to me, but after that bonfire, he ripped the C right out from his heart. Maybe Danny had something to do with it, but why should I care?

We're out of the clicky club. We've graduated high school and can live our own fates. I never knew we were going to see each other again, even if this world is the size of a dust particle.

The coaches arrive from the treetops. Two Hunters march out from under the Grotto, splitting up to their side posts. Commander Moriz walks out of the cave with her heels clapping against the natural stone. She sets down a few sheets of paper on her podium and prepares herself. Our teams watch as a river continues to flow between us. Everyone stays silent as the birds tweet to one another in the high trees. A squirrel scurries up one of the trees. It climbs onto a branch and sprints to the end of it. With all its might, it takes a heaping leap off the branch as it soars through the air. It lands on another tree branch and scurries inside of a hole.

"Wow!" Commander Moriz says. "It's been three days and look where it has gotten us to. I have to say, I'm impressed with you guys. I don't know if it's the coaches or what, but this is sleeker than my supposition."

"What does supposition mean?" Shawn says.

"I don't know," Eleven says. "Now shut up."

"I congratulate you boys on the accomplishment of your training," Commander Moriz says. "After learning the skills of team bonding, teamwork, and individual assessment, you'll now soak your skates on frozen waters. It's time to put your skills to the test. We have a hockey arena out in the forest; The Den. Your teams will be chunked into five different groups. There will be a few leftover, which means you may have to double up. You boys will be scrimmaging. Three versus three. We'll explain the rules tomorrow when we commence." She grabs her sheets on the podium and flushes them together. "Until then, we'll see you at The Den." She turns back around and disappears into the cave. The Hunters march from behind her.

The darkness fades over the lake on this cloudy night. The forest screams a silence tonight, not even a cricket rickets in the night. I lie on my top bunk looking at the cabin light. No mosquitos entertain my boredom. I tilt my head on my pillow and find Orson getting ready for bed. Thrasher's empty bunk sits from under him. I wonder how he's dealing with the days as they dash by. Thrasher has been there for him when he needed it most.

Ash rolls over on his bed a dozen times, shaking our bunk into a pirate ship on wacky waters. Behind me, Louie has taken over Barrett's spot while Barrett sleeps soundly on his bunk.

"You guys fine if I turn the lights off?" says I.

Louie looks around at the guys. "Flip the switch."

"Lit." I crawl down the side of the bunk while my hands and arms are still sore from the treetops. Calluses rip thin layers of skin on my palm like a paper shredder. I walk my stiff legs over to the front door to flip the switch. I flick the light off as the darkness fades in. My eyes try to gain focus back in the blackness, but I can't see much. I look back to the screened-in door. The blue shield isn't there. Maybe I can sneak out to Counselor Campbell's cabin.

I hop into my bed again as I wait out the drifting clouds. The clock above the door ticks the time away as the boys fall into their deep sleep. Ash snores up a storm while the others play possum.

The wind picks up outside as the trees sway their branches against the cabin's roof. The clouds cast their fast-moving shadows on the ground as they race in front of the moonlight. Before the clouds completely move away, I should sneak out and stay hidden in the darkness.

I climb down the end of my bed where our hockey bags stack. As I sneak down, I stare at Ash's snoring snout, making sure it keeps on snoring out its thunder. My foot flattens against the wooden floor, then the other. I scurry around the hockey bags and discover that my little plan worked. My hockey stick pokes out from under the door, keeping the blue shield from draping over. Looking back one more time at the sleeping beauties, I widen the door's gap and slide out. It squeaks back, doesn't flush shut, and doesn't disturb a mouse. The blue shield sticks to the top frame of the door, wanting to lock us inside, but it doesn't.

The moonlight scatters across the lake and through the trees like a bunch of missing puzzle pieces. I walk down the steps of our porch and hide beside it. I'm going to have to jump from one cabin to the next as quietly as possible. I take a few deep breaths as my adrenaline kicks in. My heart bashes out beats while my blood does the tango. With an explosion, I push off the grass and dart my way over to Cabin Four's porch. I crouch into a squat and waddle along it. When I make it to the end of the porch, I take a sneak peek over into the forest and up the hill. No signs of the Hunters. I rip through the darkness and sneak in front of Cabin Three. Their light shines through the screened-in windows and door. Cabin Three, the place where two worlds collide. I keep out of the light as I make my way to the end of their porch. When I sprint to the next porch, the clouds fade out from the moon, catching me in its white light. I need to be a ninja out here, silent like a slithering snake.

When I look up at the moon, and it looks down upon me, I realize the clouds are much farther apart. This is going to be tougher than I thought. The moon's light floods through the trees and reflects off the lake to the cabins. It's a free flashlight for anyone who's scouting. A wolf can spot me from the highest mountain top. One more cabin to go. I can make it. Just army crawl your way through the grass. I lay on the ground, check the hill of thicket, then army crawl my way over to Cabin One's porch. The grass crunches from under my elbows as they delve deep into the mucky crust. I make it to the last cabin. Dead campfires sit like graves by the lake. The Grotto is out in the far distance, hiding in the shadows. The cafeteria is dark, and in front of me is Counselor Campbell's office. He lives there. I remember seeing a door out on the side of his desk area. All I need to do is run over there and hope his door is unlocked.

I pop out from the porch of Cabin One. After peering up the hill, I focus my vision on the office and begin to pick up my walking speed. My arms swing into pendulums as my legs trudge along its path. I'm getting closer and closer to the cabin. Almost there. A stick breaks out on the hill. I gasp and freeze in shock, staring into the shadows of the thicket. I'm a deer in headlights. Nothing moves around in the plants. I hear a swoosh through the woods. Something thuds against my arm. I shake the tremors out.

An arrow scraped the side of my arm. More sticks crack in the woods. I turn around and sprint to the cabins. As I run away from the Hunters, I hear a rustling in the plants from behind the cabins. They're chasing me. I flash by the cabins one by one in the white moonlight. The speed in the shrubs picks up as I approach my cabin. I fly up the stairs, open the screened-in door, and shut it flush, removing the hockey stick. I step back from the door and wait for the Hunters to climb up the steps with their bows, but no movement fades into sight.

Ash pulls his chest out of bed. His sheets rustle. "Liam? What are you doing?" I bolt my head around. His eyes drop to my bleeding scrape which gushes onto the floor. "Geezes." He scrambles out of the sheets and rushes over to me. "Guys." He flicks the cabin light on. Louie lifts out of bed and notices my bloody arm, and Orson wakes up wiping his eyes. Barrett sleeps like a still skeleton.

"Geezes, Liam," Louie says.

Orson discovers all of the blood. He slams his hands against his eyes and covers the view from the flooding blood. It seeps through the cracks of the floor and drains to the dirt.

"How did this happen?" Ash says. I hear static slide by my ear as the blue shield blocks the door and windows. "Liam?"

"Counselor Campbell," says I. "He wants to help us."

"Help us? With what?"

"He wants to help us escape."

"I told you. They're treating us like animals."

"Wait a second," Louie says. "How can we trust him?"

"I don't know," says I.

Ash grabs his sheets and starts wrapping it around my wound. He tightens a few knots around it as the cuff cuts the blood circulation. "I don't know if this'll hold."

"Wait," Louie says. "I have a medical kit in my hockey bag." He jumps from his bed and passes us to the hockey bag stack.

"Why do you have that?" Ash says.

"Got into a lot of fights in high school." Louie hands Ash the medical kit.

Ash rips out the gauze from its plastic. He unwraps the sheets which soaked up a lot of blood. Before wrapping the gauze on, he pours alcohol from a mini bottle in the kit onto the wound. I clench my teeth so much that my jaw can just shatter into pieces. Fire burns inside of my arm as ants crawl their way to the wound. Hornets dig their stingers down into my arm. Ash finishes wrapping all the gauze around it. "Okay. Since it's not too big, I think it'll hold, but that was deeper than I thought."

"Dude," Louie says. "You're lucky a Hunter didn't kill you tonight." He chuckles. I sneak in a smile, but I lose it.

My vision fades out as my head falls to the side. My eyelids droop as my mouth props open. Ash takes his hands under my armpits and keeps me up. "Help me move him, Louie." Louie picks me up from my feet. They drop me on Ash's bed as I fade into a deep sleep.

SWIRL

Water bubbles out of a pan from the stovetop like a summer hot spring. Steam rises into the air and smears upon the microwave with its sauna-like heat. The water bubbles so high that drops fly out from the pan like a volcano and land on the hot stovetop. One of the worse smells in the kitchen has to be burnt water. But that's why you don't fill the pan all the way up to the brim. Okay, that may be an exaggeration, but the water should only go halfway max. It's thrilling to think that the smoke alarm might go off from burnt water, but it doesn't seem like it'd go off because burnt water doesn't release smoke but stinky steam.

Mother takes out a box of mac-n-cheese from the cupboards and places it next to the stovetop. She uses her nails to tear open the first flap. The cardboard flap rips in half. She pries her nail under the bottom flap and rips the cardboard off. She takes the cheese packet out of the box and pours the macaroni noodles into the boiling water. The timer is set for seven minutes. She clicks start, and it begins counting down.

A big plastic spoon sits on the countertop by the sink. Mother grabs the spoon and stirs the noodles in a merry-go-round. She looks into the whirlpool as the center of the hurricane hollows deeper and deeper. Then, she switches her stirring direction and deflates the whirlpool. With the timer at six-in-a-half minutes, she places the spoon down on the countertop. She walks over to the sink and washes her hands. She looks out the window at the backyard forest. It's too dark to see anything, the moon shimmers past the treetops as their tips stab into the night sky. She turns the water off and flicks drips from her fingers into the sink.

A kitchen towel hangs from the oven's handle below the stovetop. Mother dries her hands, then searches for the time. In neon green lights, the microwave reads 1:50 am. She looks at the white wall phone over by the refrigerator. With the mac-n-cheese at five-in-a-half minutes, mother decides to pick up the phone and dial. The phone gives its monotone hum. She stands in the lit kitchen; the dining room is lit too, but from the kitchen, a staircase leads down into the dark half-basement, and then another staircase around the corner leads to the full basement. Behind the refrigerator wall is the normal stairs to the bedrooms. Mother looks down into the darkness listening to the hum. Her body starts to lighten into a feather as goosebumps tickle along her spine like a vine wrapping around a tree. Her toes tingle into fizz. She takes a deep breath as the phone reads off a message: "Hi. This is Liam. Please leave a message."

With a robotic beep, mother hangs the phone up on the wall.

She bites her lip and watches the timer countdown from four-in-a-half minutes. She walks back over to the hot springs and stirs the noodles more. While she swirls the noodles, she thinks about calling again, but she knows it's two in the morning. She's been trying all day though. No one has been picking the phone up. She probably knows nothing is wrong, but a mother will always wonder and worry.

Mother finds her purse on the dining table. She ravages through it in search of something. She pulls out a business card. It presents the phone number and email for Steve, the bus driver of the Great Griffin. She takes the card with her to the wall phone and dials his number at two in the morning. The phone hums and hums and hums as the darkness from the stairs taunts her again.

The phone clicks on. "Hello?" says Steve.

"Steve," mom says. "Hey, this is Jenny, Liam's mother."

"Jenny. Hey, what's up?"

"Well, I've been trying to call Liam's cellphone, but he hasn't been picking up."

"He's probably not receiving your calls. They're in the middle of the woods, and there's probably no reception in that pit."

"Possibly, but it's been ringing. Liam's usually good at picking up phone calls."

"I'm sure everything's perfectly fine."

"I know. I just miss him so much already. It's hard living in silence."

"I hate to bug you, but would you like some company?"

"You're not bugging me. If anything, I'm bugging you, calling at two in the morning." Steve chuckles. "Maybe I do need some company."

"I think that would be best for you."

"Where and when should we meet?"

"Your choice. I'll drive down to you from the cities and meet you in?"

"Kielstad."

"That's right. The Kielstad Knights. I've always loved that name."

"I'll take you to the pizzeria in town here. Shall we say six o'clock in the evening?"

"That should be perfect."

"Sounds like a plan."

"I'll see you tomorrow, Jenny."

"See you tomorrow."

THE HIKE

Breakfast is a quick one this morning. Me and Barrett want to take our walk around the lake on the hiking path before the big ceremony with Commander Moriz. Pancakes and bacon glorify our noses as we slam them down. I'm not too fond of maple syrup, but there must be some amazing maple trees around here because it hits different. This syrup must be fresh from the northern maple trees. Once I chow down my food, me and Barrett head out of the cafeteria and to the hiking trail, right between the Grotto and the round lake.

The sunshine beams down upon us again, and the leaves look greener than ever. The humidity is perfect while it's not too sticky. Birds tweet their messages again through the branches, and a chipmunk scurries in the brush on the ground. I love escaping out into nature. Nothing beats the tranquility and quiet like the woods. Forests just give me good vibes, and I think it's because I've lived around them my whole life. I always love to go hiking, and once in a while, I'll go mountain biking on some roller coaster trails. And the best part is that I get a workout while having fun.

The trail seems quite dry after a few rainy days. I'd expect more mud than dirt, but I guess it all probably drained in the lake. The trail loops around the backside of the lake here which is where our canoe challenge ended. It's quite a flat trail following along the shoreline of the lake and a huge woodsy hill. There's no doubt that Hunters are up in the trees at the top of that hill. It's the perfect overlook of the lake and Camp Kelmo. It's unbelievable how they imprison us in this camp. I still can't believe that incident from last night with the bow. Are they going to hurt me now? Am I in trouble? What would they do to me if they caught me sneaking out again? Whatever it is, I just hope it's painless. I've dealt with enough pain in my life already.

Barrett stumbles over a tree sticking out its roots.

"You okay?" says I.

"Yeah," Barrett says. "Got a little dizzy there, but I'm fine." We keep on walking down the dirt path in the shaded woods. "Do you think I'll be alright?"

"Is that even a question? You're a hockey player, and you're one of the toughest hockey players I've met. This concussion, it'll be gone with the wind." Or at least I hope so. I know how high the treetops course was, and that could have killed anybody. I'm happy Barrett's still alive, and I'm happy he doesn't have to wear any casts.

"You know when I said I didn't want to go home ever again?" Barrett says.

"Yeah. Did you change your mind?"

"I don't know. I feel like I should want to go back, but then a part of me doesn't want to leave you. I'm having a blast with you and the boys, but I don't how I feel about this place."

"This place is dangerous, and it's totally normal if you feel confused right now. That's something suffering does with us; it confuses us to the point where we just want to end our lives. Ever since high school ended, and with every day passing by, I've been feeling empty on the inside. It feels like a fresh start, but then I always find myself questioning my life and why I'm even here."

"I stress myself out over my dream, and my school for that matter."

"What's your dream?" Barrett hesitates to say something. He chuckles to himself too. "What? What is it?"

"I want to be a pilot."

"Oh my gosh. That's an awesome dream, Barrett."

"But there's one problem."

"What's that?"

"I'm afraid of heights."

"What? Wow. Okay. After we get out of here, I'm bringing you to an amusement park, or to the cities and go inside of a skyscraper. I'll bring you to the Foshay Tower and we can go on the roof and look over the edge of the viewing platform."

"Maybe. I don't know if I'll ever get over my fear of heights."

"Barrett. Would you do it if I was by your side?"

"If you're by my side, I'll definitely consider it."

"I hope so. Fear can haunt a person for the rest of their lives, and it ends up killing people's dreams. You need to learn to face your fears or else you're just letting the darkness consume you."

"You know what? You're right. We are going to do this THIS summer. We're going to get out of here, and I'm going to have a blast with you."

"This'll be the best summer yet." I'm happy to see Barrett in joy. It's been so dark and depressing around here lately. But what about me? Barrett has himself figured out, and I know I wanted to be a filmmaker, but that means I'd have to give up hockey. I can't just leave my life behind. Hockey is home. Hockey is my heart. It keeps me thriving every day.

"What about you, Liam?" Barrett says. "What do you want to do in your future?"

"I don't know," says I.

"Do you have a fear? Does something scare you?"

"I'm sometimes nervous about things, you know? Never scared though. I don't know what terrifies me. I feel like there's something, but I can't lay a drop on it."

"Maybe you're scared of yourself?" He has a point. Maybe I am scared of myself. I don't have my life bundled up. It feels like my mind is just in the middle of the woods, stranded in the middle of nowhere with no path to follow. There're too many choices for my future.

Life after high school kind of sucks.

We curve around the lake as we're heading back to our cabin. Ash, Louie, and Gray rush out of the water, ripping their towels out of the sand and running back to the cabin.

"Guess we should get ready for the ceremony," says I.

"Do you know what the ceremony's about?" Barrett says.

"Not sure. All I know is that it's critical for us to be there."
Now that I give it some thought, today's the day we hop on the
ice. Commander Moriz will explain what horrifying drills we'll be
experimenting in, or maybe our hockey sticks will turn into
swords and axes as we fight to the death in the arena, inside of The
Den. Whatever it is, I'm not looking forward to it. And maybe
that's normal for summer hockey. Like I always say: *It hits
different.*

GONDOLA

Our hockey bags have been stanching up the cabin, but it's about time we start using them. With my hockey bags slung over my shoulders and hockey stick in hand, I lunge down the porch steps and meet the others at the campfires. Other Team Ink members leave the cabins with their equipment as well. It appears they taped their sticks already. Black tape. It makes sense that Team Ink will probably be team dark. Ben's head must be poisoned with anger. He's going to hate how much black he has to wear, especially after all those high school years of wearing a blank canvas. No more white for you, honeycrunch.

While we march along the grass road, sticks clank against one another. From behind, fishbowl Shawn and Eleven sword fight with their hockey sticks. I'm shocked at how Shawn is walking down the porch backwards and doesn't even look down for the steps. He seems to be a master at going backwards. Maybe Shawn should be a defenseman and not a centerman. As they proceed onto the path behind us with their dramatic war, we cut through the campfires and join the rest of Team Frost at the Grotto. Coach Hill and Dr. Fallenhein stand side by side to the right of the Grotto's podium. They tower over us, and Team Ink's coaches tower their team on the left side of the podium. Gray, Louie, and Ash chit chat to each other. Eli and Viktor doze off, eavesdropping into Team Ink's conversations. Shawn and Eleven finish their sword fight and merge into our pack. Siv arrives with his bulky pads dangling off his goalie bag. Goalies deserve more appreciation with those military packs. It's like they're carrying a dead buck.

My hike with Barrett this morning has lessened my worries with the ceremony. It was a nice calming walk through the woods and along the shoreline. I keep thinking about what my future will hold. Where will I go to college? Am I going to make it to the college leagues? What will I be studying? Will I dorm with one of my friends? Will they be going to the same school? I don't know what I'm going to do, but it was nice to get Barrett's insight into his dream. A pilot sounds like an awesome occupation. He's going to make bank in his future, but I can't bear the thought of all-nighters while trying to keep the plane functional. I can't believe he's afraid of heights though. I feel so bad for him now. The coaches forced him to climb onto the treetops with no safety net. I wonder how the other boys were feeling through all of this. I've always remembered Eleven's fear. His name is literally the number that looks like a pair of needles. 11. Ugh, that number always pricks my skin. Shawn's afraid of spiders. Orson doesn't like swimming. The other guys probably have relatable fears, but how about Ash? He's been my best friend and teammate since day one, and I can't seem to find his fear. He's never really been scared of anything. He's a tough guy, and he's going into the Army. Something has to scare him, worry him at least.

While we continue to wander in the woods, I realize there's still a missing piece. Thrasher. Ever since the Hunters took him away for not giving his phone up, I haven't seen him. Counselor Campbell might know where he's at. I miss hearing Thrasher's voice. He was the chill guy of the group that everybody liked, even Orson appreciated him. But ever since I met Thrasher, I swear I've seen him before. I don't know where.

Heels click upon the Grotto's rocky floor as two Hunters divide out from the cave. Commander Moriz struts to the podium and organizes her papers. Everyone quiets and waits for the ceremonial speech to commence.

"Good morning, Camp Kelmo," Commander Moriz says. "This is a big day. Today, you boys will be stepping on the ice for the first time. The Den has been waiting for you all. Many people will never get to experience this arena as you will today. This is a very special arena, there's nothing quite like it. You boys will be facing each other in a 3v3 scrimmage." No way. I've always expected camps to mainly focus on our skills while we'd do the same drills. At least in high school, the drills were set on repeat. "The games will be thirty minutes long. Team Ink and Team Frost will be broken into five sections. The goalies will play in each scrimmage, and three boys will continually compete. There'll be a five-minute intermission for a fifteen-minute safety." Why am I not flabbergasted that this camp needs to have a safety in the middle of a hockey game? "I was approached by one of the coaches that the teams are unbalanced. So, I got a bowl here filled with names from Team Ink's roster. Coach Hill will do the honors in selecting a player to switch teams."

This is not happening. My bet is there's only one lucky name that'll come out from that bowl. Out of their sixteen players, it's going to be him. This is going to be hell. He hasn't been supporting our team at all. He's never liked me for whatever reason in the past. He's going to make our team a failure. And when he makes new friends on my team, he's going to rip them from my hands.

Commander Moriz makes room for Coach Hill as he walks to the podium. He reaches his hand inside of the glass bowl and pulls out a slip of paper. "Blain," Coach Hill says. Team Ink turns their heads to him. He stands beside Ben. He gives Ben a fist bump, then gets a pat on the shoulder from each of his fellow teammates. I don't know how I feel about an outsider, an enemy, joining our team. This is high school hockey all over again. We're going to be fighting two wars at once; the game itself, and the clickiness between us.

"Great," Commander Moriz continues. "Now, your teams will have five equal sections." Not true. We'd have a complete team if Thrasher were here. "Now, all that's left is our ride to The Den." How are we getting there? I really hope we're not walking there. The Great Griffin isn't in sight.

Commander Moriz, her two Hunter guards, and the coaches lead us out into the woods. We walk through the brush while branches catch my bag and scratch my legs. We crunch the dead brush as a deer jumps out from behind a tree. We amuse the sight of the doe as it gallops away from us. Sweat dampens my forehead, probably making my acne worse. I never cared for my skin. I believe hockey can be a little to blame for. I hate those days when the air just dries my eyes out into a frozen plain. Exhaustion isn't the ideal thing you want when skating in a fast pace game.

In the middle of an open, grassy terrain, a rectangular station sits. There're no train tracks on the ground, but ziplines direct my eyes from the station to the other side of the woodsy hill. It's a steep climb, one that a person would have to use all fours to climb. Mountain climbing gear would be the way to go for that hill. This ride isn't a train. It's a gondola. Silver cars float above the green trees and crank around in the station.

Commander Moriz takes us to the station as we all hold our hockey bags, ready to jump inside the moving cars.

"Two guys per car," Commander Moriz says. "Team Ink will go first." She hops into a moving car with two Hunters by her side. The doors seal shut as her car boosts up the hill and into the tips of the trees.

"Why does Team Ink always get the benefits of going first?" Barrett says.

"I don't care to be honest," says I. "It just means they'll have to wait for us at the top."

"True. Do you wanna ride with me?"

"Yes. That would be awesome."

The line moves quite fast as the cars roll in one by one. Team Ink's final pair hops into the car and rides off. Ash and Louie are next in line.

"I don't know how I feel about a scrimmage," says I. "I don't know if I'm in shape or not."

"I think after the challenges, we're probably in good shape," Barrett says.

"Probably. But we haven't done any sprints or anything."

"We should do warmups before the scrimmages."

"Yes. Good idea. If you don't stretch, you might not have a good performance."

"Or you might tear something."

Me and Barrett find ourselves next in line. A car swings around and slows for us. We throw our hockey bags over our shoulders and into the gondola. We use our hockey sticks to pull into the car. We sit side by side in the car as the doors seal shut. The sound of nature turns off as the silence of the electric gondola pushes off with speed. We rise as the trees shrink. The car passes a support beam as the gondola rocks us like a sailboat on the high seas. Me and Barrett lock eyes and chuckle. Barrett's fear might be eating him up, but I hope laughing is his medicine. Out the windows, we watch the beautiful hills of green crest over each other. A crow makes a figure eight in the sky as it swirls above the woods. A fly buzzes inside of the gondola. Barrett keeps looking forward to the top of the hill, hoping to find the end.

We make it to the top of the hill, but it's another support

beam. The gondola rolls down the hill and brings us to the end where a huge building rests. It's a perfect rectangle. Modern. No windows. Just an exterior of cement tanning in the hot summer sun. Right across the top of the doors displays the name of the building in blue.

The Den.

THE DEN

The ice is small for a typical 3v3 scrimmage, or even goalie and individual training. There can be sheets of ice anywhere in Minnesota; rinks on the frozen winter lakes, inside of a barn, one in the basement of a suburban home. The opportunities are endless in the north. This rink feels oddly familiar. It gives me the feels from Peewees when we played teams all over the cities. The arena mimics the Minnetonka Ice Arena, and not the classy arena where the high school boys and girls play, but the older arena the younger ones use. The ice is definitely smaller, but the concrete bleachers match up. The majority of the bleachers sit on the left side of the rink, over by the scorebox and penalty boxes. In the front here, right next to the entrance, is an old, concrete seating area made of blue scummed-up plastic benches. Behind the player's benches are four sets of small concrete bleacher blocks. Two of them are placed behind each bench, and they both split down the middle to make a corridor in between them. This is where we'll be running out; through the corridor, onto the bench, and leaping onto the fresh, crisp ice. On the far wall, way at the end of the arena, is the zamboni room.

Commander Moriz and her Hunters stand to the side as our coaches lead us to our locker rooms. Team Ink walks all the way down to the other end to find their locker room. Ours is behind the first bench. Coach Hill opens the door and holds it open. As I follow the boys into the room, Dr. Fallenhein glimmers his teeth at me in a happy orange peel. We enter the locker room and find a spot to drop our bags and sticks. I find a spot in the middle while Ash, Louie, Gray, Viktor, and Eli take a seat in the back. Max and Miles plop down in front of me. Barrett takes a seat next to me, then Orson follows next to Barrett. Shawn and Eleven are near the front. Siv takes his front seat by the door while his gear steals most of the floor space.

Blain, the new guy from Team Ink who's forced to join our team, comes inside last. He drops his bag in the front corner of the room and avoids contact with anyone. It appeared he and Ben were friends, close friends. They gave each other a fist bump, but everyone else just patted him on the back, wishing him good luck. All I know is that he needs to contribute to our team. He may be another Ben from another team in the state. Almost every team feels like a mimic of ours. There are always the goofballs, lazys, speedsters, BEASTS, and no team ever seems to be missing them. But don't forget about the drama that kills the team.

Dr. Fallenhein seals the door shut. The locker room is like an ice cube as we're all trapped inside the brisk. It feels good to be out of the heat and back inside the cooler. Coach Hill pulls out a whiteboard marker from his thin coaching jacket. Dr. Fallenhein still has his fancy black lab coat on, and I can't forget those LED glasses of his. On the whiteboard, coach writes down a list of our team, showing the times of the five games. He saves our names for last on the whiteboard.

A knock at the door interrupts Coach Hill. Dr. Fallenhein pulls it open. A Hunter stands back by the concrete bleacher blocks. A boy protrudes in front of him. It's Thrasher. He walks inside with his gear as the boys around the room murmur. Ash tells Thrasher to take a seat by him. The boys ask him questions, but coach starts his talk.

"Alright," Coach Hill says. "Our team is divided up into five squads. Five games. Three men, and Siv, will play in the half-hour matches with one fifteen-minute safety. The winners of the game will be fed dinner, and the losers will have to wait for their next opportunity. This is how the rest of camp will go. You boys will be scrimmaging each other every day as we teach you new skills, techniques, and discipline. So, if you're worried about your health, you should probably take these games seriously." How can these people be so cruel? Starving teenagers because they lose in a hockey game. "First Squad: Gray, Eli, and Viktor." Gray high fives the Russian Elites. "Second Squad: Liam, Thrasher, and Barrett." Thank God. I grab Barrett's hand and squeeze it in excitement. "Third Squad: Eleven, Louie, and Shawn."

"Let's go, baby!" Louie says. Shawn rips his shirt off and twirls it in the air like a helicopter. He howls.

"Alright, then," Coach Hill says. "Fourth Squad: Miles, Orson, and Max." I wonder how the Barrier Brothers feel about this. Since the cafeteria, I've been drowning in their story about their abusive father. Actually, I bet this camp is bringing it all back to them. They've been forced to starve. This is not what hockey's about. "Fifth Squad: Ash—" Coach looks down at his sheet of paper. "Blain." He's missing one more guy. "It looks like we're going to have someone double up. Let's see here. Liam. You'll play two scrimmages today." Why me? How am I ever supposed to ditch this place? How am I going to run away? I bet my beanie hats that they're torturing me for that little scenario I played that one night. Can they blame me for sneaking out? It's kind of their fault for not having the shields turned on around our cabins in time. "If you guys aren't playing, either sit and watch the game or do your warmups inside. No one leaves the rink till we're all finished playing."

Dr. Fallenhein pulls out a duffel bag from outside the locker room. "Take these, boys," he says. He gives us a plastic bottle filled with a dark blue liquid. "Drink these before you go out on the ice. I need the bottles back before the first game starts." Some kind of energy drink. Barrett pops his cap off and chugs a quarter of it down. Orson sips on it with two hands on the bottle. I twist mine open and give it a whiff. Smells like some kind of fruit with a heavier presence of a chemical. I gulp down a puddle of this blue liquid. It tastes like a thick grape with a little hint of blueberry muffin. I gulp down another pond and find myself addicted to this drink. I chug down the rest of the bottle. As I go bottoms up and finish the drink, drips of it streak down my chest. I rest my empty bottle on the bench and chap my lips. The drink flows down my body and pools into my stomach, refreshing like a dip in the lake on a hot summer day.

I turn to Barrett who pounds the rest of his drink. "Shall we venture around the rink?" says I. "We have about an hour."

"Yes," he says. "Orson. Come with us."

Gray, Eli, and Viktor beat us out the door for their warmups. I lead Barrett and Orson around the concrete bleacher blocks to the doors we entered through. Two Hunters block the doors with their crossbows in hand. I curve with the boards to the old bleachers. They stack up high to the wall, a total of ten concrete slabs. I follow the boards to another curve which leads to the main bleacher section. They tower over us as they're close to kissing the ceiling. Behind the bleachers is an open but dark corridor. It kind of reminds me of the endless hallway at The Barn, but there's more air flowing through. It's an invisible river of air. The bleachers split in the middle where the scorebox sits. We walk behind the scorebox and find the stairs to the bleachers. We rest on the stands in the blazing cold.

Something's odd with the scorer's box. The penalty boxes have built-in glass ceilings. Hockey boards with glass also split the penalty boxes from the scorer's station. Must be a way to protect the players from raining popcorn, or even worse, a twister of nacho cheese spiraling on top of their helmets. The rest of the arena seems pretty simple. The lights blind the ice with a blasting white, and the scoreboard is a small square, hanging above the zamboni door. But confusion concusses me, and it concusses Barrett even more. Two mops swing from the bottom of the hockey boards on the ice and connect into one by the goal line, paralleling with it. It's a long mop, resurfacing the ice. I've never seen anything like it.

I'll never see a zamboni mop the same ever again. My mind flashes back to The Barn. Ben and Danny trapped me inside the zamboni cellar. It pulled out of the room while Charlie broke his ankle. The zamboni crushed him with its mass and squealed his skin like it was a dimpy little rug. All that blood that splattered on the boards. The wall was a white canvas being splattered upon in red paint. Then the ice soaked in his blood as the zamboni resurfaced. And the worse part of all: me, trapped in the cellar, staring straight into Chester's peeled off face with intestines dangling out from him. I'll never forget that horrid smell of fresh, heated meat. It was like a deer being cut open with its blood gushing all over the ground. Fresh, bloody venison with a hard punch of zamboni fluid.

Music electrifies the stadium through the speakers on the ceiling. The quality is so much better than The Barn. They give a deep rumble of thumber in the arena while a ceremonial song plays. They're timpanis, marching drums, cymbals, and even a chorus singing. Not your typical warmup music, but I guess the boys are still stretching. Not a huge icebreaker at the moment.

The mop finishes resurfacing, splits back into two, and tucks away inside of the boards. The ice is as crisp as an autumn apple.

After a while of chilling on the bleachers, Squad One hops

onto the ice. It's game time. Team Ink and our squad circle around the zones and wait for pucks. Two Hunters skate on with normal zebra cake reffing clothes, and they got crossbows slung to their backs. The ceremonial music keeps playing throughout warmups, then pucks slamming across the glass riles up. Once in a while, a special *ting* will ring the arena.

Counselor Campbell appears at the bottom of the bleachers. He hops up beside me and sits. "When do you play?"

"I'm Squad Two," says I. "And Squad Five."

"Coach doubled you up?"

"Yeah." I pick at my fingernails.

"Shit."

"What?"

"How are we going to get you out of here?"

"I don't know. What was your plan?"

Barrett turns to us. "Wait. What are you talking about?"

I turn to Counselor Campbell. "You can trust Barrett. He's with me on this."

"Well, my plan was for you guys to sneak out of the arena. There's a small town not far from here. It's about a twenty-mile hike through the woods. All you'd have to do is follow a downstream."

"Twenty miles?"

"I know it's not a walk in the park, but it's better than being here."

"Wait. Can you call Steve and ask him to drive the bus here? We can sneak on the Great Griffin and he can take us home."

"I don't know if we can trust him though."

"You can trust him. He likes my mom."

"Are you sure you feel comfortable with this?"

Glancing at Barrett for his approval, he nods. "Yes. We're comfortable with it."

"I think I can get this done tonight then."

"That would be awesome."

"Maybe we can get your whole team on board with this. But for now, stay quiet. They're listening to every conversation they can. So, after your first game here, I'll hopefully have a plan with Steve. You guys should prepare on sneaking out later tonight."

And with that, Counselor Campbell leaves us. The two Hunters blow their whistles as the game is about to start.

SWITTERED

Max and Miles hop on the bleachers, joining me, Barrett, and Orson. Out on the ice, Gray battles the centerman at the faceoff dot. Eli and Viktor are probably going to be jumping back and forth between forward and defense, all three of them perhaps. 3v3 is a different game of hockey. There's really no defense, and you need all three guys to accomplish anything on the ice. We need to win these games too or the camp will starve us to death. Five games today with five squads, and why do I have to double up? Hopefully, me and Ash can work together. He seems to have mixed feelings with me. It's like his mind's a smoothie, blending up the good and bad. He was mad earlier about how I stood up to him about giving this camp more time to reveal itself, but I should have trusted and listened to him. He's also going into the military after this. He probably notices all the militia-like training in Camp Kelmo. On the bright side, at least he'll be prepared for the Army.

Team Ink dumps the puck into our zone. The two Hunters

wear crossbows on their backs while they stay along the boards, moving with the puck and following the game. Eli picks up the puck in the corner and skates around the net, looking for a breakout. Viktor stands in front of the net like any other defenseman would do. Gray positions himself on the weak side of the ice, over by our bench. Eli skates the puck north as Team Ink pressures him toward the boards. Eli prepares for a hit and whips the puck into Team Ink's zone. The puck whirls behind the opponent's net as Gray picks it up by the hashmarks. He takes a nice slapper at the net as the goalie blocks the shot and covers it. A Hunter blows his whistle for stoppage of play, but since this is 3v3, there are no faceoffs. The time keeps counting down, currently at 28:58. The boys have a long way to go. The goalie on Team Ink passes the puck to one of his players. They push our guys into our zone. What sucks is that Team Ink has two goalies that'll probably switch every other game which is a huge disadvantage for Siv.

Ash, Louie, Shawn, and Eleven chill on the smaller blocks of concrete bleachers behind our team's bench. Coach Hill yells at the guys on the ice from the bench about their defensive positions as Dr. Fallenhein scribbles notes on his clipboard. His black lab coat sways in the breeze from the skaters racing by. Team Ink throws a hard wrist shot at Siv. The puck whizzes by his goalie helmet and slams against the glass. Two guys in black pressure Viktor down low while he protects the puck with his body. He backhands the puck to the other corner where Eli stands. Eli grabs the puck and skates north. He looks across the ice where Gray speeds into a bullet train. The other two players who were battling with Viktor backcheck the puck.

Eli and Gray are on a 2v1. Eli slingshots the puck to Gray. Gray speeds the puck around the defenseman. He fakes a shot to the left as the goalie drops to the ice. He slides the puck to his backhand and topshelfs it. Team Frost is up 1-0. No time for celebration. Team Ink resumes play from their zone as our guys back out for another day of defense.

A figure pops out from behind the scorebox where Commander Moriz sits with her two Hunters protecting the door. It's Thrasher. He lunges over every other step and takes a seat.

"Dude," Barrett says. "Where have you been?"

Thrasher's silent. He watches the guys battle in our zone.

"Liam," Miles whispers. He leans into me as his cross-necklace dangles over my arm. "I recognize that look in him."

"What do you mean?" says I.

"Our abusive father always found a way to shut us up. Whenever he would give us a yelling after a game, me and Max would always avoid eye contact with him and block everything out."

"Like the silent treatment."

"Not exactly. It's more like you're forced to stay silent. We call it Swittered; isolated and tortured till you feel alone and helpless."

"How did your father torture you guys?"

"Mosquito spray in the mouth. Sleep outside in the blistering winter with no jacket. Force our hands onto red stovetops. He'd tear me and Max apart to make us feel alone. Some of the times, Max and I would fight each other over our father, wanting to be his favorite so he would hurt the other more."

I can't even imagine what kind of father would do that to their own children. If Thrasher is going through the same thing, Camp Kelmo definitely has a stricter system of Swittering. There's no way they'd just keep him a few days for little luxuries. He's completely oblivious to us. He only focuses on the game in front of his eyes. If he was isolated for a few days all because he wouldn't give up his phone, I can only imagine what they'd do to me or Barrett if they caught us escaping camp.

Whistles scream on the ice as Viktor and a Team Ink player punch each other in our zone. Gray dissolves into the fight, trying to break the guys apart. A Hunter ref skates to them and breaks them apart. He squeezes onto the opponent's jersey as the other Hunter glides to Viktor. Both Viktor and the other player are brought into the penalty box. They take a seat in their glass cubes. I wonder if the penalty box is like our school bus sauna rides, trapping all of the humidity inside without a single cool breeze.

The timer on the scoreboard stops. Commander Moriz beeps in their two-minute penalty. The Hunters prep for another faceoff at center dot. Now, it's a 2v2 for Gray and Eli.

The ref blows his whistle. My eye catches an illusion inside of the penalty box. A blue laser rises from the floor inside of the cube. The laser blankets the ground, acting like its flooding the inside and drowning the players. The blue blanket rises and rises as the players dissolve and disappear. Commander Moriz resumes the timer as the ref drops the puck. The 2v2 is set in motion. Back in the enclosed penalty boxes, the boys have vanished. I can't see them. Is the glass just a weird reflective mirror? Did they teleport somewhere? Why does it matter if we see them or not? All I find is the same empty penalty box as before.

"Did you guys see that?" says I.

"Yeah," Barrett says. "Weird."

"You guys should probably warm-up," Miles says. "You guys are on in like thirty minutes."

He's right. This isn't like high school when you have an hour or two to prep for the game. These are thirty-minute scrimmages, and these are games we shouldn't be late for. Besides, Second Squad on Team Ink stretches by the zamboni door. Me, Thrasher, and Barrett leave the guys and head behind the big bleachers.

"This should be a good spot," says I.

The three of us start stretching. The most important thing to stretch in warmups is the legs. I do a set of lunges, then side lunges. A few sprints and cherry-pickers here and there for cardio. I set my hands on the cold concrete bleachers to sturdy myself for leg swings. Once my legs are nice and warm, I sit on the frozen bare floor and twist my hips.

"Alright," Barrett says. "I'm good if you are."

"Yeah," says I. "You good, Thrasher?" He nods. "Okay. Let's head to the locker room."

As we make our way around the bend to the wearing-away bleachers, I find Counselor Campbell walking out the doors on a phone call. He's calling Steve. The Hunters flush the doors shut

168

once he exits. Before the concrete bleacher blocks protrude the view on the ice, I freeze and get a glimpse of the game. It's 3v3 again. Eli looks fine, but he's totally out of breath. The score is 1-2. Team Ink leads. Our team dies of exhaustion on the ice. They have nineteen minutes remaining.

Our locker room sits in silence as the other guys watch the game. The game fades out as the door shuts behind me. The locker room beautifies my nose with stale sweat and frozen tears. I zip my bag open as the trapped heat slams into my face. Memories melt my brain with the photo I found in my bag earlier. Can't believe I have to say we were friends back in the day. It makes me feel old to say *I wish I was back in high school.* Days are different without Chester in them. He's not here anymore. He's gone. I'll never be able to pass the puck to his stick. I'll never feel our gloves bumping each other after a game-winning goal. His voice fogs in my memory as time pasts. I can't bear living without him.

Life sucks.

CLICK CLACK

Me, Barrett, and Thrasher await in our gear for game time. I'm
wearing my thick astronaut suit from high school, new skates
though, and we wear our new sleek ice jerseys. My helmet lies in
front of my skates. My body heat rises through my jersey and up
to my face like a toaster oven. Stench from the frozen high school
sweat slithers into my nose. As cold as it is in the rink, it's a
volcanic chamber in here. I'm sweating with my squad as we wait
for First Squad to finish their game. I'm thrilled to get back on the
ice and tear it apart, but my mind wanders to the penalty box. The
blue blanket laser just dissolved the guys. I don't understand
where they went, and I don't know what it does. With the way
Camp Kelmo has been punishing us, I don't think I really want to
find out. It all started with canoe cross, then laser lag, and then
tipsy treetops. And Thrasher, taken from us and isolated for his
well-being. Miles called it Swittered. I never knew how many
guys actually dealt with that on a daily basis. I know there are bad

people out there, evil people, but I never thought they'd be affecting my friends' lives. My teammates.

The buzzer blares through the arena with the end of the game. We grab our helmets and pull them on our heads. The inside comforters squeeze my head. I leave my mouthguard on the side of my cage. But a part of me wants to bite down on that chewed up mouthguard; I imagine my teeth sinking deeper and deeper into its rubber jello. My father would always get mad while I'd chew my mouthguard into an overgrown bush. Rubber vines would dangle from my guard, disgusting some of the girls in the stands, but I don't care for their click. Dad had to buy a new mouthguard for me every other month though. He'd be scared that I'd get in trouble with the officials if I didn't have a "proper" mouthguard in. As long as we don't have to pull the neck protectors out. All they do is choke us while on the ice, and hockey's a dangerous sport. If anyone has a problem with their kids being chopped to pieces, then why did you sign them up for hockey in the first place? This sport is meant to be physical and for the tough. You shouldn't walk in thinking your kid is going to be entirely safe in the rink.

Now, kids should be demolishing each other on the ice, not the coaches. Commander Moriz made a camp to do exactly that, killing hockey players. It takes me back to high school. Coach Kipp used us as his pawns. We were his chess pieces, and he thought every move and every decision needed to be played correctly to win the game. But that's the thing, he assigned us which pieces we were. I couldn't even present myself as a player to him that first game of the season. I should have fought him on the bench. Maybe then Finn could still be alive. I should have done something earlier. I should've been there for him the whole entire night.

Gray checks the locker room door open as he cheers in joy. "It feels great to be back!" Eli and Viktor enter from behind him. They all walk over to their bags and rip their helmets off.

"Did you guys win?" Barrett says.

"Tied the game," Eli says. "2-2."

Viktor's drenched from a downpour.

"Viktor," says I. He looks at me. "What happened in that box?"

"I don't want to talk about," he says.

"I've been trying to get him to talk the whole game," Eli says. "He doesn't want to relive whatever happened in there."

"What do you think it was?" says I.

"Not sure. I'm kind of sick after chugging down that blue energy drink from before."

"That wasn't an energy drink," Viktor says. "It's a homogenous mixture of chemicals. That's what made me dissolve—" He stops.

"Viktor," says I. He shakes his head.

Coach Hill pops the door open. "Second Squad. You're up."

I slide my hands in my old high school gloves; maroon, black, and white. Thrasher's gloves are the Dragon's black and orange, and Barrett's are plain black and grey. I grab my hockey stick from the bench supports behind me. I lead Barrett and

Thrasher out of the locker room door. A concrete bleacher block stands tall in front of me. I turn left to find the split between the two blocks which creates the corridor to our bench. The blinding lights shimmer through the bleacher's safety rails as I pretend to fist bump the fans. Coach Hill and Dr. Fallenhein stand on the bench, waiting for us to run out. The bench's door opens right to the ice. My mind skips around as I find myself sprinting on the ice and skating around our defensive zone. I encircle Siv and his net as he stretches in the crease. Barrett and Thrasher speed around the zone with me. Team Ink hops onto the ice. Their coaches had a pile of pucks waiting for them already. They grab the pucks like hungry hogs and whip them at the net.

Team Ink wears black as we wear blank white. We were actually given white breezers to match our jerseys and socks. It's a snowstorm versus a thunderstorm.

Ice and Fire. Water and Oil. Frost and Ink.

Rock music with a touch of sci-fi ambience rumbles the arena. It reminds me of The Burg. All we need now is a dark room with fluttering LED lights, blinking across the room in a dancing butterfly show. Coach Hill dumps the pucks onto the ice by the bench. I steal a bullet and fire at Siv. It *tings* off the pole and flies over to the boys on the bleachers. I discover Ash's group moved to the big bleachers with the other guys; Louie, Orson, the Barrier Brothers, Shawn, and Eleven. The Russian Elites and Gray must be in the locker room still. But Blain, our new soldier, chit chats with Team Ink on the other huge concrete bleachers. He's talking with Ben and another kid, making fun of their guys' shots on net.

The scoreboard buzzes.

Already? We barely got to shoot pucks on the net. The Hunters check the nets and their pegs as me, Barrett, and Thrasher throw pucks into a bucket on the ice. Team Ink mops the pucks over to us, then they leave for their bench's prep talk. It makes me mad when they think we're their maids. They'll probably want us to lick their skate blades clean too. I'm pissed already and the game hasn't even started. We're going to win this game. I'm going to shove that puck down their throats, and they can suffocate on it. Just kidding. I'm not actually that harsh, but I will win this game.

No more black bullets lie on the ice. Coach Hill doesn't really have a pep talk for us. We move to the faceoff dot with Team Ink mirroring our moves. I coast to the center dot as Barrett takes right wing and Thrasher stays back on defense. The Hunter rolls up to the dot. Siv and the other goalie smack their sticks on the posts. They're ready. The ref blows his whistle. I discover the arrowhead from the Hunter's crossbow staring at me. The puck drops.

My head whips back as Team Ink's centerman smacks my head in his physicality. He turns his back to me, passing the puck to his defenseman. Barrett charges at the defenseman. The puck slides over to a far side wing near my team's bench. I target him. I skate and angle on the guy. I smack him into the side of the boards as his stick smacks the puck out to Thrasher.

Thrasher finds Barrett cherrypicking on the far side of the ice. Ink's defenseman bends his knees on center dot to block any sort of pass. Thrasher shoots the puck at the far sideboards. The puck bounces in front of Barrett. He skates to the puck and targets a shot at the goalie. He misses low. The puck slides into the corner, a perfect setup for me. I race the guy I just recently hit to the puck. He slams me into the boards. I kick the puck back with my skate, spinning south and regaining the puck. I look across the goalie's crease and find Barrett's stick. I fake a pass to him as the goalie flinches. I snap the shot and hit top corner.

On the bleachers, Team Frost jumps and cheers. Gray and Louie yell something. No time for distractions. I skate backwards with Barrett and Thrasher, waiting for Team Ink to carry the puck into our zone. The goalie slides the puck out. Ink's centerman takes the puck as he rushes to our zone. Barrett boosts forward and loops next to the puck carrier. The puck shoots across the ice to a far side wing. I fall behind the guy, but Thrasher starts to slow him down and angles for a hit. The puck fires at Siv. He leaves a rebound open for their third guy who smacks the puck in. Fuck. I forgot about the middle lane. We always need a guy to cover a lane.

Team Ink roars as they burst from their seats like fireworks. It's the battle of the hungry now. Not just us on the ice, but the war is on the bleachers too.

"Liam," Barrett says. "Don't forget about middle lane."

"I know," says I. "I'm sorry about that."

"It's okay. Let's score another goal."

"Come on, guys," Siv says. "Gotta have my back."

I steal the puck from Siv's fat blade. "Thrasher, skate up. I got defense." Thrasher and Barrett stay close to me. The Bermuda Triangle. We charge Team Ink's wall of defense as one of their guys breaks off and aims for me. I send the puck to Barrett's stick. Barrett rushes the puck into the offensive zone by the benches. Thrasher pumps his arms and strides his legs to the net. I stay up high for a weak side pass. Barrett closes in on the net. He whips a pass to the goalie's far post. Thrasher tips the puck in.

Team Frost howls their breath in the stale rink. Louie pumps his fist in the air and rubs it in Team Ink's face. Gray joins and roots us on. Ash on the other hand just claps and watches them. Orson watches the game with a settled attitude. I'm sure he's nervous to get back on the ice. I don't know if he saw what happened in the penalty box, but it won't be an icebreaker if he doesn't get a lot of penalties. He doesn't seem like the type who'd get into a lot of fights.

Team Ink pushes the puck to center ice. I play defense as Barrett and Thrasher cover their guys. Barrett covers the puck carrier as he invades our defensive zone. The Ink player hugs the side of the boards and turns around. He uses his shoulder to push Barrett out of his way and to the net. He pushes through Barrett as I stand in bloody nose alley. He rips a shot. The puck frisbees by my head and smacks the glass. Another Ink player rolls down in the corner for the puck. Thrasher chases from behind as they skate behind the net. I block his possible pass to the backdoor guy.

Barrett's in a shoulder fight with a player in front of Siv. As they try to shove each other down, the puck passes to the guy's stick. He wrists the shot at Siv's pad as it trickles out in front of him. Siv covers the puck. Barrett's guy rolls in and smacks at the covered puck. I set my hands on his shoulder and shove him back.

One of the other players pushes me back. I shove him back too. These twigs should probably move back before I snap them.

Team Frost chants my name. They love to see a fight. I discover Gray, Eli, and Viktor making their way up the bleachers. The boys cheer as they join, but Viktor doesn't look too thrilled. Whatever happened in that box eats at his emotions. Siv throws the puck up to Barrett. I skate up the side of the rink as Thrasher hangs out to dry at defense.

Barrett slides the puck to me. I take a hard slapshot, slingshotting the puck. It hits crossbar-in.

"Holy shit," Barrett says.

"I'm just as shocked as you," says I.

"Nah. You got muscles. Don't underestimate yourself." He's right. I should give myself some credit from time to time. All those days in the high school gym with Mr. Z. All those yoga days where I had sweat storms. And all those hockey games my senior year of high school. Not to mention all the hell I ventured on.

We back out of the zone, leaving Team Ink in a pissy mood. They're yelling at their guys on the ice, and it seems the players are telling their goalie to wake up. They shuffle the puck down in a Vic formation. They turn on their turbojets and target for Siv. They act as if we're invisible and they can get through our wall. All three of us back into our zone as the puck carrier sprints down the middle like a cheetah. I pick up speed and reach my stick out to the puck, but he dangles off to the side and backhands the puck at Siv. He saves it. The guy digs his skate into the ice and sprays Siv a blizzard of cold, white fluff. Barrett steps in and bashes the guy to the ice. Another Ink player fights with Barrett. I attempt to break them from each other, but a Hunter steps in with his crossbow loaded. "To the box," he says to Barrett.

"Wait," says I. "How about him? He sprayed our goalie?"

"Would you rather have him plow through your goalie?"

"Yes." Siv rolls his eyes. The Hunter takes Barrett to the penalty box. Commander Moriz had stopped the time. Play is at pause.

Barrett steps into the penalty box. The Hunter shuts the door as the sound of hydraulics pressurizes. Above Barrett is the glass ceiling. Out on his right, he sees the boys cheering him on. On his left, Commander Moriz sits on a stool with a heater by her feet. She has a translucent, futuristic screen in front of her. It's lit with blue neon lights around its border, and it's about the size of a laptop screen. She beeps the two-minute penalty on the scoreboard for Barrett and gives the refs a thumbs up. We regroup at center ice for the puck drop. I can only imagine what Barrett's going to live through. He might come out as a different person.

The Hunter tweets his whistle. I try to focus on the task in front of me, but I can't stop thinking about Barrett. Get your mind out of the snow, Liam. We're on a penalty kill. Me and Thrasher must kill this penalty for two minutes. The losers won't be able to eat, and after a hockey game, everyone's going to be starving. Viktor's right. I can feel the blue liquid inside of me bubbling like sizzling candy.

As the puck drops on the ice, the blue blanket dissolves Barrett in his gear. Barrett watches the arena erase away as a new place fades into view. He finds himself sitting on a hard, black plastic seat. A seatbelt and harness lock him tight into his seat, and his hockey gear makes it much more uncomfortable. His skates rest on a metal floor with bolts and washers poking out. On his left, metal gates are closed, and rails divide into several sections, creating open space for a line of people to fill in. To his right, there's an empty control box enclosed with windows and a door. Barrett notices a microphone inside of the box. Further, on the right, a gate reads EXIT. His vision finishes dissolving the rink from above. A roof covers over him with green, metal supports. Directly in front of him, he encounters his worse fear. A little left turn of a drop leads his eyes to the chain lift.

A roller coaster.

He scans the empty station through his hockey mask, hoping for any signs of help. No one's in the station, and the whole amusement park looks to be empty. He unclips the seat belt from under him. He attempts to push the harness out from his waist, but it's too tight. Taking his breezers off won't do any help, if that's even possible. The roller coaster constricts him like an eagle digging its claws into its prey.

The coaster jolts forward. Barrett chokes on his breath. The wheels squeak on the green tracks as the train rolls down the small turn-hill, building momentum to reach the chain lift. His body reclines on the seat as the front of the train moves uphill. The chain pulls the train as the rollback clicks and plucks the anxiety in Barrett. The ground on his left zooms out in a fisheye effect. He flushes his eyes shut. His hands squeeze the harness where his

179

veins delve through his skin like tree roots in dirt. Click clack. Click clack. Click clack. The train goes. The wheels roll on the rickety rails as the green dies off. The wheels have worn out the tracks. Barrett feels the wind shaking the ride, swaying it from side to side. He peeks an eye open. He spots a pine tree. It's the size of his fingernail. He squeezes his eye shut. His hands bang against the harness, but it won't budge.

Barrett tilts his head to the floor and squints. He searches for a release lever, but there isn't one. Of course, a release lever wouldn't be by the passenger's feet. It's always located under the car. The coaster keeps clicking in his ears as his heart pumps faster than his blood. His feet turn into feathers as his skates push against the metal flooring. He hangs onto the harness with his hockey gloves, squeezing for his dear life. Barrett feels for his mouthguard with his tongue, then he bites on it. He clenches his teeth into the rubber, ready to scream his lungs out.

The roller coaster starts to flatten out. Barrett can't handle the temptation and pries his eyes open. The car tilts him down as he looks directly into his most incredible fear. Heights. The drop appears to lead the tracks to a long crest, but after that, a second hill rests, and the tracks end at the top.

The roller coaster holds him at the edge of the drop. Then, the chain releases the wolf. Barrett's body flies up in his seat as the wind gushes through his cage. Gravity then shoves him down into his seat as his teeth clench tighter on his mouthguard. The train whips him over the first hill as his body feels like it's levitating in the seat, but his harness holds him in. He keeps his eyes open as the train falls over the crest of a rainbow. His skates slam into the metal floor as the coaster curls up the second hill. Barrett reaches the end of the tracks. His train leaves the rails as he flies in the air like an autumn leaf falling from its dying tree. Barrett stares at the dark, fluffy overcast clouds. He stops breathing. Butterflies flutter inside his stomach and chest. The back of the train swings up to the cloud as Barrett watches the ground fade into view. More coaster tracks from the same ride catch his eyes. As the train soars to the tracks with speed, Barrett stays in silence and awaits his fate. He slams straight into the rails.

Everyone stops playing on the ice. The rink turns into a glacier, frozen in time. My eyes can't find themselves, stuck in shock. It's like everyone has been struck by lightning. We stare at Barrett who crashed through the penalty box door and slammed into our bench on the other side of the rink. I take little strides over to him. He twists his head up to the sound of my skates. I kneel on the ice. He wraps his arms around me. I lift him back onto his feet, but he doesn't break his arms. He strangles me in a hug.

"It's okay, Barrett," says I. "Everything's fine now." I caress my glove on his helmet, trying to calm him. He shakes in my hands. "Hey. We gotta finish this game." He shakes his head no. "We still have twenty minutes left. Then we can get off." He pushes away. His skates scurry over to our bench where Coach Hill and Dr. Fallenhein stand. A ref blocks his way while pointing an arrowhead at his face. Barrett stumbles back. I catch his fall. "I'm sorry, Barrett. We have to finish."

The Hunter draws his weapon back.

11

Time moves like a snail, but the buzzer finally blares. Barrett skated in circles the rest of the game while his mind twirled in fear. Thrasher's voice rests inside of a quiet quarry. It felt like I was the only one who took action during the game. I suppose I'm used to it. I put the work in for my team in high school while the first liners just wanted to make movement for the audience's entertainment. Coaches are no different in Camp Kelmo. It seems many of them bring their dictations wherever they go. Maybe the state needs to do a better job with who they put in charge, especially in this politically biased world. It's also a positive thing though. I get to learn how to talk with diverse politicians, figuring out what makes them happy and what makes them ticked. If they like to play monopoly with us, then so be it. Let's just add another battle to this hockey game. We're all trying to make it to state, for different reasons, and we all end up fighting each other in a mythical battle of salt. Three battles in one war. We might as well have a flamethrower in one hand, a machine gun in the other, and a tank controlled by our feet.

Me, Thrasher, and Barrett glide to the bench and step off the ice. Coach Hill and Dr. Fallenhein ignore our passing while they find something else to draw their attention to. Guess we did lose pretty bad. 4-11. I think. Siv's for sure gaining a great workout. While we walk between the concrete bleacher blocks, I turn around as Siv marches off the ice with his bulky pads. They must be resurfacing the ice after two thirty-minute scrimmages.

I follow Thrasher and Barrett into the humid locker room. My brain swirls as my vision draws back. I'm dehydrated. We didn't have time for a water break. I don't even know if there were water bottles on the ice. There has to be a water fountain or a sink inside of The Den.

Eleven, Louie, and Shawn are dressed for their game. Their gloves and helmets lie on the padded floor as they wait for the mop to resurface the ice. Shawn snugs his helmet on, leaving his fishbowl unclipped.

Siv pushes his pad on the door and enters the locker room. The door shuts. He falls to the bench and settles himself. He flips his helmet off and swallows as much oxygen as possible. "Geezes. I'm tired." Barrett and Thrasher stick silent.

"Gettin a good workout, huh?" says I. I unstrap my helmet and throw it in my bag.

"Yeah. Especially when I don't have my guys to back me up out there."

"You can't blame it on us. We tried our best."

"So, you guys just leave me to dry in the dirt?"

"No. That's not what I'm saying."

"That's what it felt like out there."

"Did you not see Barrett fire out of a barrel?"

"That's right. Guess I was too focused on the GAME. How bout no more penalties?"

That's one thing I do agree on. Penalties only make the game worse. "Deal."

Louie leans into Barrett. "What happened to you, sport?" Barrett stares at the padded floor while drenched in sweat.

"What?" Eleven says. "Don't speak, mate?"

"Guys," says I. "He's shellshocked right now. Leave him alone."

"That's exactly what Ash told me," Louie says.

"To leave him alone? Why's he mad at me?"

"He says you take his chances away. He feels like he needs to compete with you."

"He thinks I'm one step ahead of him."

"All the time." The buzzer blares through the wall. Louie grabs his helmet. "Let's suit up, boys." Louie, Eleven, and Fishbowl Shawn snap their helmets, slide on their gloves, grasp their sticks, and head outside in the arena. Siv lazes his way to the door and allows gravity to plop his helmet on his head. The door slams shut.

"Alright," says I. Barrett and Thrasher haven't taken any of their gear off. "Come on, guys. We need an escape plan." Barrett breaks out in silent tears, then he escalates into a breathing rampage. I hustle over to him in my clicking skates. "Barrett, Barrett. Hey." I move his eyes to mine. I stare at him without saying another word.

He starts to die down. "I don't know if I can explain what happened."

"It's okay."

"I was strapped on a roller coaster. I couldn't move. Then the tracks ended." My eyes don't flinch. My vision focuses on his voice. "It was so high. I couldn't do anything."

"Nothing?"

"I could only scream."

I'm sure that blue drink has some fishy side effects. Barrett could only scream. And it was his worst scenario to be in. He's never been on a roller coaster. He wants to be a pilot but he's afraid of heights. I don't know if his plans have changed, but that penalty box serves cruelty. Commander Moriz must be running the thing inside of the scorer's box. Now it's all coming together. The camp made us interview with Counselor Campbell in his cabin while he asked us our positions, skills, and fear. They're using our fears against us. For what though? And why us? Why were we selected to serve?

The scoreboard screams in the arena again, signaling the end of Third Groups' warmup. As the humidity makes the sweat surface my skin, I rip through my gear. Chester would always rip through his gear, faster than he could run on the track.

Barrett and Thrasher pull their upper gear off.

"Commander Moriz," says Thrasher.

I can't believe it. This is the first time he's spoken, but his throat clogs with strings of yarn, webbing out in branches, cutting his voice. "What about her, Thrasher?"

"It's her." Me and Barrett try to unravel what he said.

"What do you mean it's her?" says I.

"You guys didn't hear about her son? On the news?" Barrett shrugs his shoulders. "Annie Moriz. Her son, Clayton, was playing hockey last summer. He was hit from behind. The medics pulled him off. He's been in a coma ever since." Thrasher freezes into ice. "They showed him on the news last winter. I will never forget that kid's number. 11."

My brain bursts to gush. Commander Moriz is going to see Eleven out there. She's going to have a fricken heart attack when she finds him. She probably already has. Will she treat him like her son? Will she favor him on the ice? Or will she punish him, perhaps kill him? I can't imagine what's going to happen out there. It's hard to think that memories won't be flashing back inside of her head. She's gonna be in a wild storm.

"We need to get out of here," says I.

"How?" Barrett says. "You have to stay for Fifth Squad." Frick. That's right. Coach Hill forced me to double up. Fifth Squad: me, Ash, and the new kid from Team Ink, Blain.

"Okay. Well, we need to find Counselor Campbell. Barrett, you and Thrasher are the only ones who can escape right now without drawing suspicion. I just don't know how this is going to work with all these Hunters around."

"We're just going to leave you and the others behind?"

"I don't know about Team Ink, but if we can get Steve's bus, we can at least get our guys loaded on."

"Why do we have to escape then?" Barrett asks. He's got a point. Counselor Campbell wanted us to escape The Den, but it doesn't make sense if he's planning our escape route. Something draws my suspicion about him. I never really knew if we could trust him. He works for the camp, and he sounded so strict when we arrived. Is he lying to us? Does he want to watch us sneak out in desperation and get shot by Hunters for pure entertainment?

The door opens. Counselor Campbell enters and lays his back on the door, shutting us inside this swamp crate. "I called Steve. He's going to be here at midnight sharp."

"In front of the cabins," says I.

"Yes. You'll have to be fast."

Part of me doesn't want to believe him, but I'm torn. "How can we trust you?"

He kneels in front of me. "You want to make it out alive?" I nod. "Then trust me." He stands in front of the room again. "Barrett. The only way you can sneak out of this place without getting caught is through the zamboni room. You'll need to be a sneaky snake."

"Thrasher's coming with," Barrett says.

"Wait, Barrett," says I. "We're not escaping the rink."

"Excuse me?" Counselor Campbell says. "He needs to escape."

"We'll escape tonight when the bus arrives."

"If you want to survive, you need to leave this place."

"Which we'll do tonight."

Counselor Campbell grabs my helmet and slams it on the wall. "No! If you guys want to survive, you'll do as I say."

"Sorry, Counselor. We're done dealing with dictators." I find Barrett and Thrasher beside each other. "We work as a team. We don't leave a man stranded." Counselor Campbell clenches his teeth to a tint of red. He stomps out of the room with anger, the same anger Coach Kipp always had. It makes me lose faith in him even more. But now what will happen to our bus? Is he going to call it back? Will Steve still come and rescue us? I remember him having a thing for my mom, he made that quite obvious even if he didn't see it himself. I hope he'll help us, but I can't trust anyone who works for the camp.

"Do you think we'll ever get out of here?" Barrett says.

"Yes," says I. "We will."

I unlace my skates, pull my bottoms off, and slide my clean clothes over my swampy stench. "Imma go on the bleachers." Barrett and Thrasher continue to take their gear off. I exit the locker room to find the two teams chanting away at each other. The chirps echo through the concrete bleacher blocks. I walk towards the ripped blue bleachers near the front entrance of The Den. As I make my way around the corner of the arena, I hear a bloody scream. Eleven stumbles out of the penalty box, impaled with dozens of needles that stick out like gigantic stingers from black hornets. His fear is his number, and his number belongs to Commander Moriz's son.

11. Needles.

REBOUND

Ash fears for his new friends on the ice. Louie, Shawn, and Eleven struggle to play their game. Only five minutes have passed. First Squad. Gray, Eli, and Viktor. They're beside each other, keeping comfort with Viktor in between them. He's still hushed from whatever that box transported him to. I can't remember Viktor's fear, I don't even know if he's told me. They're the Russian Elites. Usually, others would see them as stereotypical Russians with stone minds, but I see them as human beings. They're nothing different from me. They only come from a different starting point.

Me, Barrett, and Thrasher stroll by Commander Moriz, who's still in the scorebox, and her two Hunter guards. She sips a steaming cup of coffee. We stride our way up the bleachers and settle next to Orson and the Barrier Brothers. The two bros and Orson are Fourth Squad. Their game is next. Ash sits on the far side of the brothers, keeping his focus on the game. This may be the time to talk to him. Things may happen tonight. To me, to

Barrett, to anyone. I still can't trust Counselor Campbell. He wanted us to escape The Den, but the wolves will always sniff down their cubs. They've already punished Thrasher for a simple retaliation.

I leave the guys to move on the other side of Ash. He keeps his eyes glued to the ice. I find Eleven struggling on his feet. Louie and fishbowl Shawn pace with Team Ink's game, trying to keep the score close. We're down 1-2. Eleven stops skating and pulls a needle out. It's about the size of a one-foot ruler. Over half of them aren't even a half foot deep, but maybe that has to do with the challenge inside the box. Maybe it could have been a lot worse.

"I don't want an apology," Ash says.

I look at him, but he hesitates to reflect. "I'm not here to apologize." He sighs with a deep and dramatic breath. "You were right. We should have gotten out of here when you said so." Eleven cries as he's been knocked down by a player, stabbing some of the needles through his hand. "This place is torture. I didn't realize that till now."

"It's a concentration camp. That's what it is. They work us. They starve us. What's next, Liam? What do you think they're going to do with us? Huh?"

"I don't know."

"Of course, you don't know!" I face away from Ash's spit as his voice carries into Team Ink's section. Ben and Blain sit beside each other, peering at me.

"Louie says I'm always a step ahead of you. Is that true? Do you really think that?"

"Ever since high school, Liam. You've always been the next in line. I'm always sitting in the back, waiting to be played. Waiting for coach to say something to me, something positive for once. He's never liked me. No one on the team seems to like me. And yet, you're always getting credit and leadership before me while I'm here waiting for something to happen. And you. You don't seem to have an answer for anything, but yet people listen to you. You always get the benefits, and you don't even realize it."

My sinuses clog with snot and a dreary mist. Ash never releases his emotions to me. I've always seen him as tough. He's the tough militia guy who's joining the Army next year. It seems he's been hiding his emotions for too long. "Maybe you're right." I lift from the bleachers. "I should just stop trying." Ash finds my back turned to him as I walk down the bleachers. Orson looks over to Barrett. Barrett grows a small smile, but it dies instantly.

Team Ink ignites as they score another goal on Siv. Me and Ben meet each other through the bleacher's railings. My feet freeze in place behind the scorebox. I sense the Hunters watching me, but Ben bothers me more. His flat expression gives me chills in this summer heatwave. A storm's brewin. I have to play in the last game. I don't know if I'll have the energy or stamina to do so. If I can only find some water around this place, then I can feel hydrated at least.

I head behind the bleachers and walk at a steady pace, swinging my arms back and forth. Looking around everywhere for Hunters and a water fountain makes me appear suspicious. I march by the rough blue bleachers and pass the guarded entrance. No water fountains along the walls. There must be a sink in a bathroom here. While I make my way behind the concrete bleacher blocks, cheers flood the arena. As the two concrete blocks split in half for our team's alleyway to the bench, I discover a Team Ink player escorted to the box.

I keep on track. A couple of doors sit between our locker room and Team Inks. I push the first one open as a light flashes to life. It's an empty locker room. The second door is in the middle divide of the arena. It's locked. Could be a storage room. Or the camp locked the bathroom to taunt us even more. We're the rats in their experiments. The third door opens, and the lights already shining. I peek through, wondering if this is Team Ink's locker room. But inside, three Hunters wall up Counselor Campbell. He's telling them he's innocent. That he's done nothing wrong. He doesn't know what they're talking about.

"Tell us what plans you made with the kid," the middle Hunter says.

Counselor Campbell locks his lips. A Hunter whispers to the middle Hunter. The middle Hunter shoots a bow in Counselor Campbell's head. I release the door and dart to my locker room. Team Ink continues to cheer their team on to victory.

I'm trapped. I've lost all of my friends. My teammates. Senior year of high school is rebounding.

JUMBOTRON

Ambience from the hockey game sinks into the locker room. My heart dances with my anxiety waiting for the Hunters to kill me at any moment. My skate blade is detached from my skate and in my hand. I need to protect myself. I got no one by my side anymore. Everyone's stunned, at least the ones who've played in the game. I still don't understand the fear of that box, but it does present itself on my teammates' faces like a smeared painting. Time has passed since our last meal. Guess the only drinking water we'll receive is in the cafeteria. The only other choice we got is the lake water, and maybe there's a nearby stream, but even then, the Hunters would dart an arrow through our brains.

Counselor Campbell. I can't believe I witnessed his death. I don't understand why he didn't tell the Hunters about our plan. He kept it from them, tucked away in another locker room. The plan is with me. He left me stranded, alone to fight off the camp. But he saved us from failing. The guards don't know what the plan is.

Was Counselor Campbell actually on our side the whole time? Was he telling the truth about wanting to save us? He was desperate of getting us out of here, out of The Den. I didn't trust him. But now I realize why he wanted me and Barrett to leave in the first place. They may just slaughter us before our game. Maybe even on the ice.

The door swings open. I leap to my feet with the skate blade ready to strike. Miles, Max, and Orson enter the locker room. They're dripping in sweat from their warmups. Fourth Squad. It's almost game time for them. Orson's freaked from Eleven's reaction to the needles. I'm not sure what the Barrier Bros feel about the box, but they've been through rough times. It's probably just another hike in the woods for them. They all dig in their bags and suit up.

Nothing can beat hockey. I love the gear we get to wear. No other sport equips as much gear as we do. Whenever I suit up, I feel the gravity lift from my feet as I hover in heaven. The smooth glide of my skates surfacing frozen water. The cold air seeps through my mask and coats my face in frost. The oxygen minting my breath and freshening my lungs. Every time, I feel like I'm floating in another world with my spacesuit and weapon at hand. Nothing will make me happier.

"You okay, Liam?" Miles says. His cross necklace bounces off his chest as he straps his knee pads on.

"Yeah," says I. "Everything's fine." A part of me doesn't want to explain the things that have happened, but another doesn't want Orson to hear the truth. It'll scare him. I just need to wait for

194

the right time.

"What's with the skate blade then?" Max glances at the blade in my hand. Orson's eyes have been locked on my blade for quite a while.

"Just nervous."

"The penalty box?" Max says. I nod.

"Don't be worried, Liam," Miles says. "Just don't get a penalty. That's all they're asking." Yeah. Simple. Just don't get a penalty out there. No lazy whacks with the stick. No fighting. No retaliating. Simple. Piece of cake. Piece of pizza. Piece of puck.

We stay in the tropical heat. No one wants to watch the game anymore. Third Squad finishes their game and enters the locker room. Louie's hair pours rain on the floor. Shawn's fishbowl fogs his sight. Eleven follows them, limping into the room with a funny walk. He rests at Siv's spot. A few more needles poke out. Chickenpox dots scatter his body from the swelling bruises.

Siv enters and spots a seat next to Eleven. "How did that happen?"

"The fucking Commander," Eleven says. "That's how."

"She stabbed you with needles?"

"No. She locked me in that box, and I found myself running through a rain forest as needles impaled me."

"No way. That's fricken awesome!" I've never seen Siv so impressed.

"No," Eleven says. "It's not." He pulls out a needle like it's an arrow in an archer's target block. Slowly but surely, the stinger's out and a small dot of blood leaks out from the red wound.

"I think you guys deserve more punishments for the stupid penalties you leave me to kill."

"Shut up, Siv," Louie says. "No one asked."

"I never asked for penalty kills," Siv says.

"Enough!" says I. "Siv. I know you're probably dying in that net out there, especially when you're forced to play all five games." My hand mops the sweat off of my face. "Okay. Look. I think we can all agree we need to get out of here."

"Yes," Eleven says. "That would be ideal." Siv sticks his tongue out at Eleven.

"But how are we going to get out?" Miles says. "And when?"

"There's kind of been a plan already laid out," says I.

"A plan? What plan?"

"We're breaking out at midnight."

"And when were you gonna tell us about this plan?" Louie says.

"I didn't want to speak till I knew we were in private," says I.

"Sounds like a plan Ash made a long time ago."

"I know. I was wrong." This shuts Louie up. "The Hunters killed Counselor Campbell." The boys' mouths hang open, frozen, like Danny's frozen yawn. "He was helping me and Barrett, planning for days of our escape. He called Steve. I'm hoping the bus will show up tonight."

Louie rips his upper pads off and throws them into his bag. "So, we'll be escaping at midnight tonight?"

"Yes."

"Did you tell the others?"

"No. But we need to."

"How bout Team Ink?" Miles says.

"Yeah," Max adds. "Are they coming too?"

"I don't know how we can tell them," says I. "I don't know if they'll trust us or be on our side."

"We can't just leave them here," Miles says.

"I know. We'll come back for them. But right now, they're spoiled."

"Liam's right," Louie says. "They're on their own. They won't leave. The camp spoils them."

"That doesn't mean we just leave them here," Miles says.

"They're not on our side, Miles. The refs have been calling penalties left and right for our team. They're favoring them."

"Either way, we're all going to break out," says I. "We'll come back for them. And if they really want to, they'll fight back just like we are."

Louie throws his upper gear into his bag. He unties his skates, ripping the plastic from the tips of the laces. Shawn follows him and takes his gear off. Eleven's on his bottoms. Coach Hill knocks on the door, then peeks his head in. "Fourth Squad. Let's go." Max and Miles buckle their helmets and grab their sticks. They march out of the room.

Orson waddles to me all suited up. I raise a fist to him. His knuckle fist bumps me. He leaves the locker room and heads for the ice.

"Here we go again," Siv says. He drops his goalie mask on

197

and exits.

"Is there any water in this shindig?" Shawn says.

"I searched The Den," says I. "Our best chance for water is the lake."

"Damn. I'll have to fill my water bottle before we leave." Shawn better stay silent about the plan. The last thing we need is the Hunters ready to strike at midnight in an assault.

Third Squad proceeds to take their gear off. I peek in the arena behind the concrete bleacher blocks. No suspicious Hunters stand outside. It's the same two that have been guarding the front doors to the gondola. I push in the hall and head to the others. Gray, Eli, and Viktor are ready to go back to the cabins, but they know they must wait for the games to finish. Thrasher and Barrett watch the game with their heads on their hand supports; elbows on knees and head resting on vertical arms. Ash watches me walk up the steps again. I give him his space, hoping his anger has plunged away.

Me and Barrett sit on the outside of Thrasher. We both scout Orson skating around the defensive zone. The Hunter refs blow their whistles, commencing the game. Team Ink and Team Frost take their places on the center circle. The goalies signal the refs. The puck drops. The boys battle. Miles wins the faceoff and passes the puck to Max. Orson plays defense.

"Can't believe you have to play another game," Barrett says. "Are you ready for it?"

"Nothing's worse than back to back games in high school," says I. "How's your head?"

"Throbbin like a heart. Feels like my brain is hardening into a boulder."

"I was scared for you. After you crashed into the boards. Thought you'd be paralyzed."

"Like the Commander's son."

He pops a thought in me. "Do you think that's why she's doing this? Torturing others because of her son's event?"

"Makes sense. She's hurting us like her son's hurtin."

"I wonder if she feels guilty about it."

Team Ink flares in yells from the stands. Orson lays on the ice from a big hit in neutral zone. Max and Miles carry the puck deep to the net. The puck fires at the goalie, but he blocks the shot. The puck trickles into the corner as the tides turn. Team Ink pushes into our offensive zone. Orson's back on his feet in a 2v2 with Max. Miles backchecks to the zone. Team Ink passes the puck across the zone for a one-timer. Siv swipes the puck with his glove. He drops the puck for his team. He knows the drill. The time continues to run, and the Hunters want play to resume speed.

Orson skates with the puck while Max and Miles interweave and switch sides, confusing Team Ink. A player charges at Orson. He flings the puck to Miles before he's slammed into the ice. The Team Ink player scurries back into the zone. Orson wobbles back to his feet. He looks at the refs for any signs of a penalty. None.

The puck bounces off the glass. Team Ink pushes north again. Orson shreds backwards as Max and Miles keep up with the puck. Team Ink whirls the puck around the boards in defensive zone. Their far side player picks it up on the other side and wrists a hard shot on Siv. Siv deflects it with his leg pad as it rebounds out front. Orson finds the Team Ink player that slammed him down chasing for the rebound. Orson bends down, protruding Siv's point of view. The guy slaps the puck. Orson blocks the shot in the shin, missing his knee pad. He falls on the ice as a burning blob attracts his blood like bees and honey. He pushes his weight on his stick and skates the pain off. We howl for Orson as he goes back into battle.

Miles dangles the puck around a Team Ink player. Miles and Max have a 2v1. He skates the puck in and sends it to Max's stick. His brother one-times it. *Ting!* The puck ricochets off the side post and flutters into the corner. Max checks a Team Ink player in the corner, fighting for control of the puck. Orson stays high in the zone where a defenseman usually stands. Miles jumps into play with another Team Ink player. It's 2v2 in the corner. It's a wolf brawl. Sticks smack and smack at the puck as Max protects it with his skate. Orson skates to the boards. Max finds him from the side of his eye and kicks the puck out. Miles flings the puck up to Orson. Orson sprints the puck to the net. He fires. He watches the puck tick the inside netting as the Team Ink player pounds his body into Orson. They both crash on the ice. Orson's head bounces off the ice like it's a trampoline. The Hunters tweet their whistles and hold their crossbows out. None of the boys attack each other in a fight. Team Ink yells from their bleachers, wanting a fight to break out. We wait for the next victim to enter the box.

Before I can even guess what Team Ink's light punishment will be for that hit on Orson, I discover the Hunters pulling Orson to the box. They're giving Orson the penalty. Three guys stand tall on the ice for Team Ink. My boys yell from the bleachers at the blasphemy. I can't find my words, but the anger and anxiety build inside. I know Orson's fear. He can't be in there alone.

I set a foot on the lower bench, starting to make my way down the bleachers.

"Liam?" Barrett says. "Where are you going?"

I look back at Barrett before taking off. I sprint to the scorer's box area and aim for the door. The far Hunter points his crossbow at me, but there's no need in using it as the other Hunter tackles me to the ground. Commander Moriz spins around in amusement. The Hunter picks me up and faces me to her powdered face.

"What are you gonna do to him?" says I.

"Wanna see?" Commander Moriz says. She presses a button on the paused scoreboard. The scoreboard pushes out from the wall and divides into two equal sections. A jumbotron floats out of the wall and sits in the center of the scoreboard.

"Don't let him go alone! Let me in there."

She looks at both Hunters, then back at me. "Take him to the locker room."

"Yes, Commander," the Hunters say.

"Lock it up."

"No!" I cry. "Orson!" Orson watches me from the box in his spacesuit as I'm pulled away from a new set of Hunters, potentially the same Hunters that slaughtered Counselor Campbell. Commander Moriz turns her back to me and resumes the game. I catch the box transporting Orson in the blue laser blanket to his fear factor. He begins to fade away. The Hunters pull me by my arms behind the huge concrete bleacher as my legs drag. We approach the rough blue bleachers as I struggle in their grasp. But when I find Orson on the scoreboard, my body becomes limp. The colors dissolve on the screen. There's a summer shade of sky blue. Cloudless. White flour powders the ground. Orson's skates sink into the flour. Thick greens of palms and plants poke out from the island. A few palm trees point to another island across the dynamic bluebell waters. Saltwater.

Orson's about to face his ultimate fear.

THE TROPICS

I watch Orson's emotions sink in the sand as I'm being pulled away to an empty locker room. He's frozen on the tropical beach in his gear. Swimming's gonna be a lot harder for him, but he's not moving. What if he doesn't swim? Will he still make it out? What happens when the time runs out for his penalty? Before another thought tortures me, Orson has found the answer. A huge wave rushes through the island of lush palms behind him. It crashes into him. He swirls around the water like the inside of a washing machine. Bubbles fizz around his ears. He kicks with his skates, feeling for the surface with his gloved hands. He opens his eyes in the burning saltwater and finds his stick floating to the surface. He grabs it and reaches out of the water. He's in the middle of the two islands.

Another wave approaches from the first island. He paddles in the flow of the waves. He kicks and kicks with his skates, but he doesn't seem to be going anywhere. He's stuck in a doggy paddle, moving only so slightly to move a few feet. There's a minute and a half on the scoreboard for his penalty.

The Hunters unlock the locker room door behind the bleacher blocks.

"Let go of me!" says I.

"Oh, we will," says the Hunter.

"Let me see the rest."

The Hunter unlocking the door turns to him. "Let him see."

The Hunter pulls me near Team Ink's locker room. I can't see the others with the concrete blocks in my way. Orson struggles in the water. He keeps his face above the surface as he kicks and kicks in the water. He's going too fast. Me being a lifeguard, I know when someone is drowning, especially when one doesn't know how to swim. Orson doesn't even know how to do a back float. The water layers a thin coat over his face as he sinks, but he kicks himself above the surface again. He chokes on the saltwater and tries wiping it from his eyes.

The wave behind him smashes through the last trees. It'll crash into him within the last forty-five seconds of his penalty. His paddling slows down. He calls for help, but no one's there to help. I watch his last few seconds of energy drain down into the depths of the ocean. The wave swirls behind him. It catches him as he releases one last silent howl underwater. The jumbotron bubbles up in the tropical water. It switches to drone view as the wave crashes into the other island.

A door smashes open in the rink.

"Let me see him," says I. The Hunter drags me around the

concrete block. Orson lies on the ice in a puddle of saltwater. Sand sticks to his skate blades. He's motionless like a dead fish on the shoreline.

The boys on the ice freeze play. Miles skates to Orson and lifts his chest up. "He's not breathing," Miles says.

The Hunter drags me behind the block again. "Please! Let me help him. He needs CPR."

"You should have thought about that before you attacked," says the Hunter.

I cry out for Orson as I see Miles through the split in the concrete blocks. He stops resuscitation. He backs away from Orson's soaked body. The refs lift him on his skates and pull his limp body off the ice. The light fades out in the black locker room as the Hunters close the door and bolt it shut.

BLOODY BRAWL

Once again, the darkness floods around me. Commander Moriz murdered Orson, even if it wasn't with her bare hands. I thought I was doing the right thing. Attacking the box in an attempt to save Orson. Creating a road map for our team's escape. But after all of that, I feel the plan was totally unnecessary. I should have known I wasn't going to break through the Hunters. They have more power than any of us. We can't outrun them. We can't beat them. They have us trapped. I'm trapped in the blackness, and it only reflects the pallor body peeking at me through a concrete wall. All those cords attached to his body. The stench of Chester's flesh and the zamboni oil. The dirty snow pile I climbed to move away from Finn's ghostly appearance. He wasn't a ghost though. He was alive. Finn died because no one had his back. And all I could do was watch the zamboni crush Chester's back, cracking him like a graham cracker. The squealing of the wheels ripped his skin off like a snake shedding its scales. If only someone was there for

Finn. If only I was there for Finn. He could still be alive. Counselor Campbell could still be breathing. Orson would be playing in his hockey game. But I couldn't save them. All I could do was watch. And all I can do now is wait for my time to arrive.

Light strikes through the locker room door as it opens. A Hunter tosses my hockey bag and hockey stick inside. The door slams shut as they abandon me in the darkness. My second hockey game must be approaching. The last hockey game of the night. Me, Ash, and Blain, the kid from Team Ink. At this point, I believe it doesn't matter if we win or lose. Team Ink already has two points from a win. Squad Four lost a super soul, and now it's just the two of them with Siv. Max and Miles, the Barrier Brothers. The only thing that will drive them to victory is anger.

I reach for my bag in the darkness. I pull it over to the bench. Night vision won't be necessary for changing. One thing Commander Moriz may not know is how smart hockey players are. We solve things in a matter of milliseconds. Our reaction and response times are faster than lightning. Strapping on gear is something I can do in the back of my head. I feel for the velcro on my compressions and slide them on. The long, plastic knee pads. I strap their velcro straps around my legs. I pull the hairy cotton socks over my kneepads, then the bulky breezers around my waist. I discover the detached skate blade at the bottom of my bag from my incredible protection plan. I attach it back in the skate with a click and slide both of them around my foot. Double knotting in the dark, even a sieve can do it.

I plop on my chest and elbow pads and throw on my Team

Frost jersey. For the first time in a long time, I miss my number being on my back. #21. It feels like forever since I wore that jersey. The Knights logo on the front with the cross, the smooth symmetry of black and white and maroon, the fresh flat ice in The Barn. I miss it all. I miss the boys, even the ones I didn't have a stellar time with. Why do I miss the hate? Why do I miss the drama? They're the things that killed our team, the things that killed my friends. The suffering sucks, but I want to live my childhood again. Sometimes, I forget my age. I'm still a teenager, almost to the new decade of ages, but I'm still a teen, and I need to live in the present. I know I have a long way to go in life, but so much has happened already. How much more can I really take?

Suicide's not an option. I'd never think about death. I'm not afraid of dying. I don't even know what my fear is. Counselor Campbell tried to pry it out from me, but I don't even understand my life as a whole. My favorite color bounces back and forth, white to maroon to mint green, I can't figure it out. I can't solve the equation of my journey. I had a great childhood that melted into a mixing pot of burning tar. The darkness of deaths, blood sauce from Chester, cold water from Finn, and black ice from father; it all bakes my meal of misery.

The Den wakens into a storm. The boys are cheering from the stands with the blare of the scoreboard. Squad Four's game has ended. I strap on my helmet and plush my hands inside of the gloves. I click my skates and feel for my hockey stick. The absence of light reminds me of my first year of Bantams. Before dad would release us onto the ice for game time, we turned the lights off in the locker room and sang our battle song. The energy flew inside of us like we were the glowing lightbulbs in the blackness. Butterflies would tingle in our legs and flutter in our stomachs. I'd catch myself forgetting how to breathe, forgetting that I'm human. We just focused on the task ahead of us. The crowd of wolves howling for their pups to win in the arena, powerful pups. The old Roman days with the fights in the coliseum. A battlefield. We're going to war, and we cannot let the enemy win.

Colorful language echoes through the locker room door. Team Ink boys yell at the Barrier Brothers. I know that anger. The anger of agony. Loss of the ladder. Rumbles from a quake. Team Frost must have won the game. How would the brothers have pulled that off with the two of them? Did Team Ink lose a player, or did the anger fuel the brothers?

The door pushes me back. I stand in my spacesuit with my stick's grip buried in the floor. A Hunter gestures my leaving. I walk out of the locker room as the lights blind me with their rays. The cold has gotten colder. I find the split in the concrete blocks and sprint over the bench and onto the ice. Ash and Blain shoot pucks at Siv. I steal a puck from the low corner and curl around with crossovers. I snipe a shot and hit Siv in the facemask.

"Dude," Siv says. "Watch it."

Dude. Did you forget my name?

I curve with the corner again and face the other team. Ben. He's skating like a crazy concord in warmups. They have a drill that flows between the three of them. He fires the puck at his goalie. He doesn't even watch his shot to see where it goes. He never notices anything. All I know is it's time to show him up. He's been treating me like trash. And now his friends look at me the way he does. Ben wants everyone to turn their backs to me for his entertainment.

The buzzer finally goes off. It's game time. Me, Ash, and Siv are the only ones cleaning the puck-littered ice.

"Looks like they don't care to help," Ash says.

"Yeah," says I. "Ben's friends never care."

Ash leans into me while we chuck pucks in the bucket. "Let's flip him over the bench."

"Ash. As much as I want to, this camp is trying to kill us. We can't afford a penalty." And if Counselor Campbell didn't call Steve for an escape tonight, then we're stuck here. We can't lose. "We have to win this game. Losers starve."

"I don't think you care about that." What does he mean? "You want to beat Ben. You want to win this game to show him up."

I close my lips. He's right, and I didn't see it myself. Guess it's better to hear things from someone else than admitting them. "Maybe you're right. It'd be the best thing to happen this summer."

Ash chucks the last puck in the bucket. He stands and reaches a hand to me. "Let's go pound him into the ground." He plants a smile in me. I'm sure he's talking about winning the game and not actually slamming his head into the ice.

This is going to be the scariest game of my life. Ben and his new posse on Team Ink. The penalty box that turns our fears into a reality. I can't imagine what would happen if I were in the box. Nor Ash. He's always the tough guy. I don't know what he's afraid of. I doubt it's the military, he's anxious, not scared. And I grew up with him. He fought in The Barn with me, fighting off the sustenance. But everyone has a fear. What is his?

The Hunter refs blow their whistles together. Team Ink lines up on the center dot for the puck drop. Blain glides to center ice in front of Ben. They fist bump each other. Coach Hill and Dr. Fallenhein ready up with fresh coffee cups in their hands. The steam from the coffee smudges the glass behind them.

"He's not going to be center," Ash says.

"I know," says I. "You want me to take center?"

"I think you should. I'll stay on defense at first. I don't trust Blain."

"I'm with ya on that." I glide to Blain as he stares me down with Ben. They both angle their chests to me. "I'm center, Blain."

"Blain's center," Ben says.

"Was I talking to you?" His cheek muscles wrinkle. I turn back to Blain. "I'm center."

"I got here first," Blain says.

"Okay, and?"

"I'm center."

"No. You're not." The ref interrupts our convo. He says the game must proceed, but I'm not letting that happen. Blain's going to play against us and jump teams. Commander Moriz understands. "Don't you Commander Moriz?" I raise my voice for

211

the boys on the bleachers to hear. Commander Moriz stares in my direction from the protective box. "Unfair teams? Favorites? Home ice advantage?" She doesn't whisk a whisper. Instead, she smirks.

The Hunter ref blows his whistle and drops the puck. Ben wins the faceoff. No different than high school. He can only win the battles that are handed to him. Team Ink rushes the puck to our zone as me and Ash defend. Blain joins Team Ink. 4v2. Siv's gonna have a blast. They form into an umbrella, passing the puck across the top of it. Ben slides closer to the net. I target for Ben's stick. He shoots the puck to the low corner where Blain stands. Blain flicks the puck at Siv. Siv blocks the shot. The puck rolls into the corner. Ash races a Team Ink player to the puck. They push with their shoulders to win it.

Ash hollers to me for help, but what can I do to help? If I go in and support, the other Team Ink player is going to jump in. Then, we leave Siv stranded on an island with Ben and Blain, unless the two were to turn him to their side. But Siv wouldn't betray us. I know him.

The other Team Ink player jumps in and steals the puck. He skates deep in the low corner as Ben and Blain close in on me and Siv. I slam my hips into Ben's body, throwing him back into a small stumble. He pushes me with his stick against my spine. He constantly hits me like a toddler kicking an airplane seat. He has no muscle though.

"Can't get around me, huh?" says I.

He slams his stick harder into my spine. I almost eat the

snow, but I catch my balance and continue to fight him. The
carrier throws the puck in front of the net to Blain, but Siv sticks
his fat blade out and blocks the pass. The puck trickles in front of
my stick. Ash and the two Ink players are off to the side. I grab the
puck and one-eighty around Ben's body, shoving my shoulder into
his waist.

A clear runaway presents itself. It's time for a breakaway.
Ben and his posse chase me down the ice as Ash stays behind on
defense. Three of the guys backcheck me while one cherrypicks
near center dot. I cross the blue line into Team Ink's zone. Their
goalie gradually backs up into the net, ready to receive his wound.
Ben smacks his stick at the back of my legs, but I keep rushing
forward. I move to the side on my backhand as the goalie follows.
I shred the ice with a turn and move to my forehand. The goalie
moves to the left as I wrist a shot to the top right corner. The puck
hits the netting for a goal.

My boys from the bleachers go wild. The Barrier Bros hug
each other and do bunny hops. Gray, Eli, and Viktor applaud us.
Eleven, who has the red chickenpox spots all over his body, and
Shawn, are yelling at Team Ink's bleacher. Barrett, Louie, and
Thrasher sit next to the standing wild boys while clapping for me.

Ben yells at his boys to get their heads in the game. He whips
the puck out of the net for Blain to take it north. Ash skates
backwards as a defenseman as I backcheck Blain along the boards.
I turn on turbo speed and slam Blain into the glass, right in front of
Commander Moriz. Clean check, and they know it. The Hunter
refs don't have an arm up. Good. Or else I'll be flipping one of

them over the boards.

Blain flicked the puck into our zone when I checked him. Ash targets the puck in the far corner. He turns with the curve of the boards and carries the puck up. He raises his head and meets Ben's eyes. Ben pounds his elbow into Ash's mask. Ash falls on the ice as Ben picks up the puck. I skate and skate towards Ben as he approaches the net. Ben snaps it at Siv. I crash into Ben's body, sending him on his knees and into the boards.

From the side of my eye, I see a ref's arm raise in the air, and I know what that means.

"Wait!" The ref taps his earbud. He listens to Commander Moriz's voice. "Let them play." The ref takes his arm down in a jiffy. No one noticed it but me. It happened so fast. He hesitated his own call.

Ben's on his shins, staring at me with devil eyes. He wants payback for that hit. Ash chases the Team Ink player with the puck. The puck carrier cycles the puck on the boards to Blain. Blain snipes the shot at Siv. I slide in front of the shot. The puck deflects off my ankle bone. My whole leg numbs up. The bubbles of a lemon-lime soda tingle up my leg as the ankle decides to act like a boulder and drop me to my knees. Ben skates around and elbows me in the head. He grabs the puck and shoots at Siv. Ash blasts in from the corner and rockets Ben to the ice.

I really hope he tasted the snow on that one.

I stand on my feet and rub off the beating bruise. It throbs with the speed of my heart, but the adrenaline to defeat Ben sure helps with the pain. Ash battles in the corner again with a Team

Ink player. I sit near the crease with Siv. As long as we can keep the score 1-0, we have a good chance of winning. The scoreboard displays the time at twenty-five minutes. Ten more minutes, then it'll be halftime.

Ben gains his breath back. He pumps his arms and shoves his blades into the ice with every hard stride. He slams the grip of his stick at Ash's helmet. Ash's head slams against the glass. He falls flat on the ice. His hands aren't gripping his stick anymore. He pinches his head in his gloves as his head hides in his knees. Blood drips from Ben's black grip.

I charge at Ben and soar him into the boards. His body bends into rubber. Blain and the two other Team Ink players slam me into the glass. Ash roars in anger and tackles Ben to the ice again. It's a bloody brawl. I discover Blain's face and punch him right in the snout. The other two players continually punch me, but I ignore them. I shove Blain out of the way and meet Ben who stands on his feet again. Ash is crunched up on the ice.

"What the hell is wrong with you?" says I.

I block a punch from him. I smack him in the mask. He punches me in the gut as I grab his helmet's cage and unlatch it. I drop my right glove and pound my fist into his face. Blain takes his arms around me and lifts me off the ground, pulling me back from Ben. Ben wipes the bloodstream from his nose. He sniffles, then smiles. I struggle in Blain's hold as he holds me tight against his body. Ben unstraps my helmet. The Hunters watch in amusement with Commander Moriz. The other two Team Ink players kick Ash again in the gut, keeping him wounded. Ben drops my helmet on the ice.

"I've been waiting for this opportunity," Ben says. He pulls his arm back and releases his boney knuckle to my mouth. My nerves spread the pain around my face like peanut butter and jelly slabbed onto toast. He releases another punch into my eye. I blackout.

Someone's pulling my jersey while I watch my feet dragging in the filthy snow. Through the cage of my helmet, which they must have put back on my head, Ben and Blain and their teammates watch me being drug away. Ash limps onto his feet again. Sivs' gloves and helmet are off at center ice. He must have been fighting the other goalie for fun. Coach Hill takes the clipboard from Dr. Fallenhein's hands as I watch him snap it into two with his knee. He's pissed at my retaliation. And I know it's gonna cost me.

The Hunter refs perch my body into a limp posture in the box. My focus fisheyes as I watch them exit the box, locking the door shut. The air stops moving, and it gets muggy. Mugginess in the cold, they just don't go together. Steam rises from the sweat on my body, smudging the glass above me. On my left, Commander Moriz types in the penalty time. The neon lights shine a five-minute penalty for me. It's only me in the box, and they're giving me a minor.

Commander Moriz grabs her sheets and opens them to my file. She remembers the odd thing about me. "Well, this one should be interesting." She clicks start on the scoreboard. The game resumes with Ash in a 1v4. The boys are about to watch me on the big screen in some sort of fearful reality. It's time to discover what my fear is, if the machine can even tell that is. The blue laser light blankets beneath my feet and rises like I'm drowning in a box. Colors dissolve and pixelate around the edges. Nothing looks clear until the laser crosses my eyes and fills the entire penalty box.

I'm in the driver's seat of my father's car.

THE FLOOD

My gloved hands squeeze their roots, popping their purple color
from my skin. The blackness is back around me, fading the
absence around my father's car. The only thing I can see are the
lights inside of the car and the headlights that shine on the snowy
road in front of me. The hum of the engine fills over my nervous
breathing. The bumps on the road, the curves, it's all familiar. I'm
in the driver's seat of my father's car the night he ran into the
parked combine on Highway 21.

A fog blows out of the vents. It clouds up my view of the
road. I let go of the steering wheel and pound my skate on the
brake, but there's nothing down there. The car's going seventy
down the snowy country road. I pray for the door handle to work,
but the door won't budge an inch. The fog fills the car like a
haunted house in the fall. My mind begins to wander all around
the road. My brain throbs as someone from the inside kicks at it.
Muscles in the back of my head tighten into a tug-of-war. The

blood in my head thickens and boils as it limps to the side. The road blurrifies as the snow pours onto the car. Vomit crawls its way through my throat, ready to puke out the hollowness from inside. My lips fade away. My eyes burn and throb with my heart. I'm losing my breath. My eyelids shut.

My body jumps from the seat. I'm grasping for clean air inside the car. It's not the car though, it's my SUV. I'm parked in front of my house, in front of the open garage door. My headlights shine on my father who sleeps with his head on the shelf. The darkness surrounds again. My headlights are the only thing allowing me to see. This is the nightmare I had senior year. I know what happens, but I'm alone. My mother isn't here. I'm in control of the car.

I honk the horn. His owl eye flares open. He stares at me. I honk at him again. He closes the eye, stands up with his back facing me, then turns around and pops out his owl eyes. They glow grey. He walks forward to me. If I go backwards, the seat's going to break, just like what happened with my mother in the nightmare. If I stay, he's going to approach the door and kill me. And after seeing what Orson had to live through, these challenges will slaughter us.

I force the shift into drive. I take a deep breath, stream a tear from my eye, and floor the pedal, but there's no pedal. Fuck. I forgot about that. With a scream, the SUV jolts forward. I face into my father's owl eyes as I get closer and closer. He seems to grow taller and taller the closer I get. I close my eyes and clutch the steering wheel with my gloved hands. I scream to make the thud disappear. But all goes quiet. Everything feels like it's hovering. Fluffy clouds in the gentle blue sky. Cotton flying in the wind. A feather settled on calm waters. It's peaceful.

I peek my eye to find my SUV crashing into the wall of the garage. My body impales the windshield. I smack the ground and barrel roll in my hockey gear. Once the dizziness passes, I lift onto my feet while my mouth naturally drops. My eye catches something inside the excruciating long hallway of The Barn. A boy. He stands there with a black beanie hat, black winter jacket, and black pants. He's staked into the ground like a scarecrow. His face doesn't present itself in the dangling caged lights.

The boy raises his head as the light shimmers in his flooded eyes. Finn.

"Bring me back to life, Liam," he says.

"Finn?" says I.

"Bury me again. Bring me back."

"You're dead."

"Bring me back, Liam."

I'm at a standstill. His emotions flop as the air flexes. He bolts from his feet and targets for me. He passes the dryland room and stomps closer and closer, his steps pounding louder and louder in my ears. My eyes glue to him. I can't move. He passes our locker room door. The weight removes from my feet. I break for the game doors and slam through. I rush to the rink's door and pound on the frozen lever. My feet transition to the rough ice. I flush the door shut, and through the glass, Finn sprints past the game doors.

Creaks crawl in my head. Metal. There's a creaking and squeaking from something metal in The Barn. My first instinct is to look at the zamboni doors. That zamboni freaks me out. It will chase you, taunt you, and find a way to smear your blood on the surface. But the steel gate is closed. A deep rumble runs through the steel exterior of The Barn. It's gushing in the walls, flowing like a deep river.

Redwater explodes from an industrial exhaust fan on the wall between the zamboni room and game doors. The redwater crashes on the ground, smashing upon the rink's glass and splashing the walls. The redwater starts to flood the area. Another exhaust fan explodes from the other corner between the zamboni door and the player's benches. The redwater floods the ceiling of locker rooms 3 and 4, then falls over the edge of the walls and down to the floor. I coast back from the glass as the redwater rains onto the ice. Two more fans explode in the front of the arena. Redwater pours on both walls near the mini hallway and the front warming area.

I'm trapped on the ice. Nowhere to go. I can only wait for the redwater to flood the ice and drown me, just like Orson. I have to do something. I have to fight back. I've been waiting for too long. That's all I do. I hope and I wait and it ends up being too late. I was too late for Finn, too late for Chester, too late for Orson, too late for escape. There has to be a way to survive. But there's only one way to get out of this box. The time needs to run out.

My eyes catch the redwater rising to the glass. It fills on the bleacher's front walkway. It seeps through the gaps in the glass and the cracks in the doors. The redwater pours on the ice in little puddle pods. The red on the ice. It's all too familiar. The torture this box is bringing me. I'm not afraid of death. I'm not afraid of drowning. I'm afraid I don't know what I'm afraid of. It seems the penalty box brews my horrifying past into a mixed marvel.

The redwater rises and rises as the vents continually pour out the water. I'm standing in a giant tub with four of the faucets turned on. The only drain I can think of is opening the doors to another room. The zamboni room. The pit. There's no way I'm going in there. I'm scared to—

My fear. My fear is the pit. I guess if the penalty box doesn't know your fear, it finds it for you. It discovers it with you. I can't go down there. In the darkness, alone, trapped, tortured with Finn's pallor presence. No, I'm not going down there again. I'd rather drown and be in peace. I'd rather the zamboni pull out from its garage and crackle my spine into broken branches.

The redwater has reached the tip of the glass. And like a waterfall, it cascades over the glass and crashes onto the ice, like milk pouring into a glass mug, flowing high into a curl. As the redwater caresses my skates, an image of hot chocolate pops into my mind. The devil's hour when I had my father's nightmare, waking up and walking down the steps to make the mini-marshmallow hot chocolate. The taste touches my tongue; hot chocolate and the sweet, salty mini marshmallows melting in my mouth.

The thought relaxes me in the rushing redwater. It soaks through my gear, but it feels so soft. My mind wanders back to the lake in camp where me and Orson took our shirts off and swam with our team. The water cooling our bodies off in the hot summer sun. The wave machine that challenged us to work together for once. Maybe the challenges weren't all that bad. We learned to work with each other. We fought as a team and escaped the danger.

The redwater fills and fills till I'm halfway to the ceiling rafters. The Barn has a pointed, triangular roof, just like the farm shed it once was. This arena feels more at home to me than my real home. The absence of my dad takes a toll on me at home, and it takes a toll on my mom at the rink. But I feel like I can sense my dad sometimes inside The Barn. This is where he helped me grow up as a hockey player.

The redwater pushes me afloat at the point of the roof. The redwater gushes from the fans underwater now. The tub packs with pressure, but it'll collapse when it's too late. I float to the ceiling and kiss it with my helmet's cage. I gulp one last tank of oxygen before sinking into the redwater. The bubbles fizz around my face and through my helmet like carbonated pop. As risky as it sounds, I decide to flip my eyelids open under-redwater. It doesn't sting as salt would, but my view is tinted in red. The mini hallway. I paddle my skates and push with my bulky arms, swimming over to the door. It's still shut, even with all the redwater pressure inside. I release the last of the oxygen from my lungs. I set my hands on the door and kick with all my might. It pushes open, faster and faster. Redwater smacks through the hallway as it sucks me inside. The redwater carries me down the mini hallway to the T crossing. To the right is the hallway to the concession area, but the water crashes me past it.

Before I attempt another breath, the redwater rushes me into Locker Room One.

LOCKER ROOM ONE

The redwater plows me into the door of Locker Room One. The wave flattens out to a pancake as I lie on a sheet of ice. The lights blind me again in their fluorescent beams. A body blocks the lights. Ash towers over me in his gear. The Den is silent. He helps me to my feet. I'm back on top of my thin blades. Redwater puddles the ice, turning it into a crime scene. The rest of my team amuses me from the bleachers. Barrett hustles down, finding a way to hop on the ice. Team Ink stares as well, not with hate, but shock. Even Ben and Blain don't encounter me with bloody fists.

"What happened in there?" Ash says.

"A lot of things," says I. While I look around, it seems Commander Moriz has disappeared with her Hunter guards. "Where is she?"

"She left." What? The game isn't over, even though I'd like it to be. The scoreboard shows Team Ink scored one goal, but man, they must have fought well. Still a tie game. The Hunter refs talk with our coaches. It doesn't seem like the game is resuming anytime soon. But why would she leave? Everyone must have watched it on the jumbotron. Did something scare her? Is she planning on experimenting me in some sort of science lab? It was just memories mixed in a mosh pit. My memories. My father's accident, the nightmare, The Barn, the pit, and Finn. But with his name, I find my answer. "Oh my gosh."

"What?" Ash says.

"She's gonna bring her son to The Barn. She's gonna wake him up." Ash understands the problem when his eyes bulge.

"We need to leave, Liam."

Barrett hustles past Coach Hill and Dr. Fallenhein and shuffles on the ice. They continue their conversation with the refs. Siv joins me, Ash, and Barrett.

"Liam!" Barrett says. He wraps his arms around me. "Thank God you're still alive."

"I'll always be here, Barrett."

"Dude," Siv says. He still doesn't know my name? "That was fricken awesome."

"Glad to have you as my goalie." I pat him on the back.

"Is it escape time?" Barrett says.

"I think so." The guys want an answer from me with the strangeness they watched on the jumbotron, but I don't think I can give them one, and I don't think I'm in the mood to plan our escape. But one person should be capable of a great escape plan. "Ash." He flings his eyes up at me. "What's our battle plan?"

Ash whispers his combat plan to us. We all nod our heads. I

tell everyone to put their fists in the middle. The power rises inside of us for a classic hockey chant. We silently chant, "Beasts!"

"Now let's go get em." says I.

Me and Ash target the refs who lean on the bench, talking with the coaches. We skate and skate, the shredding of cheese awakening in their ears. They find us skating right at them. The refs reach for their crossbows, but me and Ash slam them over the boards. Their bodies plow into Coach Hill and Dr. Fallenhein. I pick up the crossbow that dropped on the ice. Ash reaches for a crossbow in a Hunter's grasp. He smacks the Hunter with his hand and rips the crossbow out. A few arrows rest on the crossbow's holder.

The two Hunters at the front doors raise their weapons at us through the glass.

"How bout the others?" says I.

Ash studies the boys on the bleachers and the ones on the ice. They're all staring at him. He yells, "ATTACK!"

Shawn yells "ATTACK," mimicking Ash's message. The boys on the bleachers make their way down and sprint to the rough white bleachers. Ben, Blain, and the other two hop on their bench and huddle behind the concrete blocks, waiting for the Hunters to catch them. Me and Ash also jump over the boards and into our bench. He takes one side of the open doorway as I take the other. We crouch behind the boards, waiting for the Hunters to run through our corridor entrance between the concrete blocks.

Barrett and Siv join on my side, ducking under the glass as well. Team Ink and our guys sprint around the bend by the front doors. One of the Hunters fires an arrow at them. They all duck as it soars past their heads. A Team Ink kid flares for the front doors and attempts to open it, but it's locked. The Hunter impales the boy's head with an arrow. His back slides down the door as his body limps to the ground. The arrow went straight through his left eye socket. The boys run back to the concrete bleachers in panic, anger, and cries.

"We have to kill them," Ash says. I think we should wait, but I'm following Ash into the corridor. He counts us down from three, then we pop from around the corner. I'm on the floor aiming at a Hunter's head, but Ash beats me to the shot. He strikes the arrow through his heart. The Hunter falls to the ground, triggering an arrow that slices by Ash's face. It barely kissed him, leaving a slim streak of red.

"Where's the other one?" says I.

Ash points behind the concrete block. I stand, then walk in the middle of the corridor. I sling the crossbow over my back and climb the metal rails of the concrete bleacher block. I swing my legs over and settle on it. Ash tiptoes parallel with me behind the bleacher. The Hunter swings around and aims his bow at me, but I find my arrow has already darted through his head. I squeeze my crossbow like the steering wheel in dad's car. The roots tighten under my skin. I shake and shiver in the cold. My breath somehow makes an appearance in front of me. It rises to the flat ceiling in The Den as The Hunter's spirit fades away. I just murdered a man.

Ash climbs up and drops my bow for me. He slings his on his back. He grabs my arms. "Hey. You're okay. Liam listen to me.

You're going to fine. It was self-defense." I nod my head in agreement. He's right. It's self-defense. I retaliated for the right reasons. He had a weapon on me and was going to pull the trigger. I had the right to stop my death from coming first. But deaths. More deaths added to my list. "Let's get out of here."

Ash hands me my crossbow. We head to the rails facing the front doors. As we climb up to climb down, someone yells "freeze" behind our backs. We whip our crossbows out and point them at Coach Hill. He has a blade lying on Barrett's neck. He contains Barrett in a chokehold.

"You don't want your friend to die, do ya?" he says.

He adds fuel to my flame. I'm not losing another man to an old one. I fire my crossbow at Coach Hill. It stabs through his neck. His hand loosens and drops the knife. Barrett pushes him down to the concrete as his neck turns into a chocolate fountain. Dr. Fallenhein watches him bleed out through his nerdy glasses. His eyes bounce to me. He's too weak to do anything.

With the last of the Hunters in The Den finished, we enter the locker room and pack our things. Me, Ash, Siv, and Blain undress out of our hockey gear. The other guys wait by the front doors, breaking the locks by body slamming into them. While it's almost time to leave the locker room, I find the need to ask Blain something.

"Blain," says I. "Does Ben still hate me?"

He folds his jersey and socks and tosses them in his bag. "He doesn't like you. I think the way he put it was, 'He's always dragging me down.'" Like a loser. A benchwarmer. I knew he never wanted to catch the disease, but high school is done. It's over. But I guess the emotions and drama live on for the rest of our lives.

The boys howl in the arena as they successfully plowed the door open. They rush in the locker rooms for their things, then we all walk out to a hot and humid sunset. The sky burns pink lemonade and yellow starbursts, fading into the blue, twinkling night. No Hunters appear around the moving gondola, but they hide in the woods, or so we were told. I remember the one night when I tried to meet with Counselor Campbell, but one caught me red-handed. We'll have to be stealthy around the camp. But they don't know what happened here at The Den.

We group in front of the gondola. I stand on the gondola's safety rail. "Guys! None of the Hunters will know what happened here. We'll be safe until curfew. Until then, stay in your cabins. Steve will drive the Great Griffin in front of our cabins, and we'll all run with our bags and bring them on with us. We need to be quick and quiet."

A Team Ink player yells, "And how are we supposed to trust him to be here for us?"

I think about Steve and my mom. I know he had a thing for her. He'd be willing to do anything for her. "I know he'll be here. Trust me."

Eli whispers to Viktor.

"What time are we escaping?" Viktor says.

"Midnight."

And with that, everyone mentally prepares themselves for

tonight. Me, Barrett, and Ash enter a gondola car and roll through the woodsy hills as the sunset fades over the horizon.

"I'm sorry for what happened in the box, Liam," Barrett says. I smile, and I don't need to explore the words for him. I give him a hug. Ash smiles and watches the sinking sunset.

It's been interesting in Camp Kelmo, but it's time to ditch this prison.

JAGUAR IN THE JUNGLE

The wood bends under my feet as me, Ash, Barrett, Thrasher, and Louie return to our cabin. Louie flicks the switch, electrifying the mosquitos that wait for their light. We toss our hockey bags in the corner. In a couple of hours, our eyes will be locked through the screened-in windows. My gut twists in decisions, but it doesn't matter. If Steve arrives in the Great Griffin, we'll go home. If he doesn't, we'll fight our way out. The nearest town may be far, but we've fought through the wavy waters, laser lag, and an unharnessed jungle gym. Team Ink and Team Frost. We had no battle. We were fighting one another. But now, we combined into one, overpowering the camp. I wish my high school team built that mentality, but they couldn't see it through their thick, salty skulls.

A discussion in the woods lit the trees on fire with brilliance. Viktor mentioned the shields around our cabins and how they'll trap us inside around curfew. But he studied the shields in his insomniac nights, and we stuck a hockey stick in the doors to keep the shield from flushing shut. I haven't had a nice rest in some time. I do miss my bed. Guess this is how college will feel. I don't know if I want to go to college now. Will I ever be able to make it through a full year away from home? There's not a lot I have at home. I have my mother who works to keep up with our survival, and my friends who support me in the unstable circus of life. I can't move away from home to make movies. I want to follow in my father's footsteps. I want to make a difference, giving grace to a hockey team of young boys. I want to coach.

To pass the time, Thrasher, Louie, and Ash deal cards on the floor. Me and Barrett lie on our top bunks head to head. His eyes poke at the ceiling above. My hand hovers above my face, holding the photo of me and Chester. I miss his presence more than ever right now. I could really use him by my side, and I don't know if anyone can replace him.

Barrett's bed shakes against mine. He sits up. "Is that you and Chester?" I set the card face down on my chest. "Sorry."

"No, no," says I. "It's okay. I miss him."

"He'd be happy you know. Proud of your fight."

I lift my eyes to an upside-down Barrett. I can't hide my smile. "He would, wouldn't he?"

"I know I'm proud of ya. I look up to ya."

I throw the blanket from my chest and twist my body to him. "You do?"

"I've never seen anyone so confident in life. Never had anyone to look up to, even my parents. I don't have strong parents, grandparents, family. It's all depression."

I feel awful that I can't find any words to fix his pain. Depression is dark. But I do understand one thing. "We learn to fight through it though. You're strong. You're an amazing friend who's stuck by my side on this rocky road. You bring hope, Barrett. And I'm always here for you."

Static buzzes from the screened-in windows. The blue shield droops down from the roof. It waterfalls to the top of the door, but it stops. The door's propped open with my hockey stick, keeping the shield from trapping us inside the cabin. If the other boys forgot to block the doors, I'm afraid they'll be trapped here, unless Steve doesn't show. Then we'd all be capped in the cabins like a pirate ship in a bottle.

The clock ticks with the buzzed shield. Mosquitos swarm around the lightbulb. I guess the door's inviting them to our hangout party. More bites spread on my arms and neck through the dark night. The guys drop their cards as Ash throws his fist in the air with a glorified victory. A hum overlaps his cheering. Flashlights shine on the grass road in front of our cabin, in front of the shimmering lake. The crunch of dirt and rocks climbs through the windows. The Great Griffin pulls in and parks in front of our cabin. It's time.

"You guys ready?" says I.

Ash answers for them all. "We're ready."

Me and Barrett jump from our bunks. I stuff the photo in my pocket and grab my bag with the boys. Ash pushes the screened-in door open. He focuses on the other cabins. Mile's head sneaks out from Cabin 4, and Viktor's from Cabin 3. Cabin 1 and 2 follow after. With the nod of their heads, the lights blacken. Ash creaks the door open. They hustle down the porch steps towards the lakeside of the bus where the double doors are located. I'm the last one as I take my stick off the ground. The other boys rush out of the cabins and into the shadows of the trees. I focus on the bus, sprint down the steps, and make my way to the door. In front of the bus, something pricks the back of my leg. It gives out, dropping me to the dirt.

Gray drops next to me. "Are you alright?" He finds an arrow in my leg. "Dear God." He twists his head around to the running boys. "Hunters!"

Everyone bolts for the bus. Arrows soar over our heads from the hilly woods. They whiz through the air with a *zhooom*. A Team Ink boy screams his voice into the dirt with an arrow in his arm. A second one impales his face.

"Let's go, Liam!" Gray says. He holds my hand. I discover his grey eyes darting into mine. "We need to go." He refreshes me to my feet as I'm limping to the bus doors. All the other guys board as me and Gray hop on last.

"Never thought I'd see you again," Steve says. "Glad to have you back."

"Thanks, Steve," says I. A robotic sound echoes from behind. I turn, watching the water recede from the shoreline. A lot of water. The tsunami's coming. The water tides into the center circle. "We need to go."

"What?" Gray says.

"The lake."

Gray notices the water receding. He remembers the canoe crossing. "Go, go, go!" he says.

Steve locks the doors. He squeals his wheels in the grass as mud spits out behind them. Gray and I fall in the aisle of the bus and slide down the slip-n-marble-slide. We pull our bags and sticks along, flying by the other boys' gear. Our feet snap around the straps on their bags. We stop in the middle of the bus where the Great Griffin flies on the ceiling to its position in the front. Dim blue and purple neon lights turn the bus into a midnight club.

Before Gray and I attempt to stand, Steve whips the bus around near the cafeteria and campfires. Hunters block his way. And in perfect sync, the machine in the lake explodes the water into a huge wave. The boys yell at Steve. He floors the pedal. The Great Griffin speeds past the cabins like a jaguar in the jungle. Mud smacks the side of the bus. The wave starts its crest, almost to the shoreline. The wave's about the height of the tall oak trees that hide the moonlight. The Hunters aim their crossbows at the bus. They fire. The bus bumps us to a float. We hover, then crash upon our bags. The Hunters jump away from the bus and sprint for the woods. We didn't hop over tree roots. They popped one of the front tires. It feels like dirt skidding against the gears, rough and tough on the bus.

Steve curves around the lake and deeper into the woods as the wave chases us. A hill presents itself, angling the bus to a slant. We slide backwards as he slams the pedal to the floor. The bus pushes and pushes up the hill with its wobbly weight. The wave smacks the back of the bus. Water leaks through the vents on the back wall, but we made it to the top of the hill. The water drains down the hill and floods into the lake again. Boys cheer and scream on the bus. Hugs are brought around as Barrett holds his hand out for me. I grab it and join his arms.

Steve saved us. "And that's skill from Steve, the bus driver." He tunes his radio to rock music as the neon lights dance inside. Bright red flames spit from the Griffin's mouth. But now it's time for a long drive. Before we close our eyes for some shuteye, Steve must know we're not finished.

"Thanks for saving us," says I.

"It's in my blood, kid," he says. "I protect my passengers."

"We need to make a stop."

"What's the destination?"

"The Barn." The place we were picked up. Maybe he had that in mind, but I had to make sure. Commander Moriz may win this race to The Barn, but she doesn't know what Hell she's getting into. How is she driving her son to the arena? He's in a coma. It's not wise to unplug his life support. And isn't he in the hospital?

Thrasher's eyes are closed. Most of the boys lie on their bags in uncomfortable sleeping positions. Ash is probably used to it, or at least he'll need to get used to sleeping on cots in the Army. I've heard stories that soldiers actually sleep on the metal bed supports without a mattress, training themselves to sleep in any environment.

"Hey, Thrasher," says I. I shake him awake. He squints. "Hey. What's Annie's son's name again?"

"Clayton. Number 11." Eleven. Needles. The number made

of needles. Eleven skated out of the box in a bush of thorns. He was the bush, thorns poked out from his red chickenpox dots.

"Is she really going to take him from the hospital?"

"No. He's not at the hospital. They wouldn't keep in the hospital. They needed bed space for other patients. Annie was devastated and begged for life support. The hospital made a deal with her, sent him home with the medical machines."

My body flops down to my hockey bag. Ash and Barrett wake up from my fall. My lungs enclose. My leg numbs with a burning sensation where the arrow sticks out. Ash hurries to my leg. He pushes his hand against my leg and counts down from three, but he tricks me, pulling it on two. Just like a deer target, he pulls it out in a firm line. The arrowhead rips some skin with it. The blood gushes onto the white marble floor. I stare at the ceiling, watching the flames dance in a trance. The soft bass from the music pillows my ears. My eyes sink deeper and deeper into the illuminated flames above. Ash reaches for the first aid box from Thrasher's hand. He must have had one in his bag from all those hockey fights in his past, or maybe it was from the front of the bus. But as my vision dissolves and fades away, I catch a glimpse of Thrasher's nervous eyes. I remember one thing from the campfire. One thing stuck out from him. He said he played hockey for The Dragons in high school. Dorcha Dragons. And those eyes. They are the same eyes that melted his tears into mine on the bench. I locked eyes with him after my penalty by Coach Kipps' feet. I never knew why he was upset, but it stuck in my mind. And now, he has the same fear inside of him. He's the shaggy hair kid from Dorcha. The one with the disgusting *21* in orange on his sweatpants. We've collided.

The scouts. Were they at the arena for our presence? Watching us? Tracking us? Selecting the few players who will benefit them in their experiments? Is this why we know each other? It could be luck in this small world, but it feels like we've been set up. My brain can't respond to the redundant questions as I lose consciousness.

A bump of the bus awakens me, startling me. Are we here? Did we turn off Highway 21 and cross the railroad tracks to The Barn? I stand to find Steve pulling the Great Griffin to the side of the country road. He puts it in park. He props the door open and heads outside. More boys wake from their slouchy slumber. We hear Steve's footsteps climbing the stairs.

"We got a flat," Steve says. He holds an arrow up. "They blew it out."

"Well," Louie says. "You gotta spare?"

"No. A maintenance crew would have to come out here."

"So, we're stuck out here?" Shawn says.

"I'm afraid so."

Complaints wiggle between the boys. Commander Moriz will break into The Barn, setting Clayton on the rink's cement surface. The rink could never afford the profit to keep a summer sheet of ice. So instead, other teams use the area for dryland and drive to Prior Lake for ice time at Dakotah. I'm scared we'll arrive when it's too late. She doesn't know what she's getting her son into. He may awaken, and she'll hear his voice again after a year in a quiet coma, but the consequences will kill.

The country road's dark. The tips of the pine trees surrounding the sides shadow in front of the moon. No one's around. No houses. No cars. Not even a nearby farm. We're still in northern Minnesota, north of Minneapolis. Not sure how close 35 is, but no lights cast in the sky. We're in the middle of nowhere, stranded. Stuck in the mud. Frozen like a glacier. Trapped in a pit. That familiar feeling. It'll never go away.

"Now how are we gonna stop her?" Barrett says.

"There has to be a way we can get to The Barn," says I.

Ben stretches to a stand. "How, Liam?"

"I don't know, Ben. You figure it out." He snickers, then faces away. "I've always been a step ahead of you, haven't I? You know, I wonder how long you wait till something is handed to you." He faces me again with salt on his lips. His tongue's not moist. He can't speak. Dehydrated in hate. "You're more of a failure with straight A's." He clenches his fist and walks to my feet. Blain and Shawn grip his arms and pull him back from me. He yells commentary at me but calms when he settles on the bench. Yet again, he's sat, warming the bench.

Even in the nighttime, the humid heat sticks to our peeling skin. Me, Barrett, and the Barrier Brothers sit in front of the bus on the road. The darkness surrounds us. A breeze sways the trees every now and then. I pinch a rock in my hand before chucking it in the pines. My stress squeezes out on the rock. Too much hangs on my head, burning my brain in flames. It turns my emotions into ashes. It'll be morning by the time anyone rescues us. We're stranded and starving. It's been a day since we've had a full meal. Dehydration doesn't help. The only fluid we got was the blue drink in a test tube bottle. The Russian Elites added everything up in camp. The frosting on the cinnamon rolls before laser lag. That's what made the lasers shock us into seizures. Seizer shocks. The blue liquid dissolved us in the box into a different world. Transported us to a deathly challenge. A challenge Orson suffered from.

A *rumming* picks my eyes from the pines. But the sound, it comes from behind the pines and in the woods. Two lights flicker behind the trees, passing them at high speeds.

"Barrett," says I. "Honk the horn." Barrett hustles to the bus horn. I sprint into the prickles of the pines and dart through the lush woods. The bus horn honks its thick accent through the dense trees. I run out in front of the two four-wheelers as they slow down in front of me. They stop. They jump off their four-wheelers as the lights shine in my eyes. As they lift their helmets off and approach me, I'm met with their voices. No way.

"Carlie?" says I. "Casey?"

"No way, dude!" Carlie says. Is everyone calling me dude now? "How are ya?"

"I'd like to chat with ya guys, but I need your help."

"Whatchya need?" Casey says.

"I need a lift." Casey and Carlie follow my path to the bus. They inspect the flat tire and can't seem to help. There's nothing nearby within a thirty-mile radius. They were just heading back to their camper after an unsuccessful day of hunting. They can't carry a busload of kids to The Barn, but a max of three people can fit on a four-wheeler.

"I wanna join," Barrett says.

"It's dangerous, Barrett," says I.

"I can handle it."

"I can't lose another friend."

"You won't lose me. And what am I gonna do if I lose you? I have no one." He's right. The only people he has are his depressants back home, but not in a real home with a roof on its head. His parents lost it.

"Fine," says I. "You stay by my side at all times."

"I'd never leave you." I squeeze him into a bear hug.

Me and Barrett climb on Carlie's four-wheeler, hanging on to her. Ash and Shawn will ride with Casey.

"Barrett," Louie says. "Stay alive!"

Shawn says to Eleven, "See ya on the other side. In Hell." Eleven laughs. They fist bump.

I glance at my constellation. My team. Miles and Max. Eli and Viktor. Gray, Thrasher, and Louie. Bruised-up Eleven. Siv.

Casey and Carlie spin the gravel to dust, boosting us through the dark vacant countryside. My wound from the arrow stings under the gauze the boys tied around it. It soaks in blood. My anxiety escalates in the everlasting wilderness. We make it to their camp where a pickup truck awaits. We hop in, squished in the back. Casey whips the truck out from their camp and speeds to our final destination.

The Barn.

VOLCANO

The hot summer heat has burned itself away. The night drifts cool air, bristling the hairs on my skin. I give my thanks and wave as Casey and Carlie whip out of the parking lot. Me, Barrett, Ash, and Shawn face the double set of french doors to The Barn. The lights are on inside. It reminds me of the nights with practices during a cold, winter twilight. Me and Ash don't doubt the possibility of flashbacks. We haven't stepped inside for a while. It's shocking to find the front doors not broken. No shattered glass. Not even a paperclip litters the sidewalk. Someone's here. There're two vehicles outside. I bet one vehicle belongs to Annie Moriz who sulks over Clayton's coma. The other one is too oddly familiar. It's a dingey, cheap car. It's always parked on Main Street in central Kielstad where the county lines split; Scott County to the North of the road where The Barn sits, and Le Sueur County to the south. It's Danny's car. Danny working the late shift on a summer night when dryland ends in the early afternoon?

Sounds like Danny, "grinding" hard during the howling hours. But I doubt Kiv signed him up for a pointless night shift.

I lead the boys into The Barn. The doors close behind the four of us. Me and Ash look around the concessions. We think about the times we've entered The Barn. Before practices. Before home games. Leaving for away games. Arriving back late at night from an away game. Tears drying out through those doors, my tears. Finns' tears. And now, my anxiety. Ash flashes back to his and Chester's conversation with Ben and Danny. Finding my beanie hat. Attacked by a wolf. Watching The Barn burn to its bits, but it didn't crumble. Its foundation is strong in concrete and steel. Everything's back to the same old. Even the screams.

Our attention draws to Annie Moriz, screaming on the ice. We bolt through the double set of doors from the warm area to the rink, the iceless rink. A section of the boards on the corner of the iceless rink has been ripped out. We cut through. Annie cries for her son's awakening. She's pinching her last crumbs of hope, not letting them drop to the dirty concrete base.

Her cries pause. Her body freezes. Motionless like roadkill. But her head, it rotates like an owl. She finds us lined up, side by side, shoulder to shoulder. "How did you get here? Who let you out?"

"No one did," says I.

"We fought back," Ash says.

"Steve picked us up," Shawn says. Barrett slaps his shoulder in grief. "What?"

"That's not possible," Annie says. "The Den had guards."

"You mean Hunters?" says I.

"How did you get through them?"

"We hunted them."

Her lips twitch a quick smirk. "Guess I did my job too well."

"You locked us in like lab rats. What made you think that was okay?"

"Kids need discipline."

"And I agree, but there's a line that needs to be drawn."

"My son's been in a coma for over a year!" Her tears construct rememberable rivers. "I wish he was dead." I understand the pain she's in. Losing someone you love. "Months after months. I wanted him to wake up for his hockey games. For Christmas. For his birthday." Clayton lies on the floor like a dead deer. "But thanks to you Liam, I found the answer I've been waiting for." What? What does she mean? Has she been waiting for me this whole time? She breaks down, but her energy and anger propel us from her bubble. "If it wasn't for you filthy hockey players, my son would be alive."

"I lost a friend last year," says I. "I lost two amazing friends. Teammates. They deserved so much more. My head aches when I think about them. My eyes drought out. I can't concentrate on anything." Her chin lifts from her soaked hands. "It's torture, waiting for a breath to lift from their lips, waiting for their stomach to rise back to life. I wish my friends were still here. I lie to myself, pretending that it was all just another nightmare, just to find that they never show up."

"But your simulation," she adds. "The boy." Her eyes dart to mine. "You brought him back to life."

"No. I didn't. I wished he was in his coffin. In peace. It wasn't human to bring him back. But it wasn't me."

"Then, who was it?"

A giant *smash* jolts our hearts through our throats. Then another. And another. The steel gate to the zamboni room shakes and rattles. The zamboni. It's reversing its mop into the door, attempting to drive through it. Me and Ash send shaking shocks to each other. The past resurrects.

The disco ball on the ceiling drops on Annie, snatching her head inside. She flops to the floor. Blood coats the shattered crystals and the concrete base. Nothing cut the ball from the ceiling, but the deflated air tube and the still ceiling fans shake side to side. The crystal pieces from the ball rattle on the floor. My legs tremble, adding tingles to the thighs. A crack crinkles in the concrete base. It slithers under Clayton's body and Annie's bloody painting. I never would have expected an earthquake in Minnesota, but it's happening.

The concrete bursts open as The Barn quakes and bakes and shakes. Me and Ash push the boys to the doors till a scream screeches from behind. Cords with needles snap to Clayton's body as he screams in pain. He's awake. Breathing. Alive. It awakened him from his coma.

"Liam," Ash says. "We can't leave him here."

"I know," says I. "You know what to do."

"We need that fire axe."

Clayton sends more screams as he crawls from the widening

crack in the concrete. His mother's body vibrates with the trembles, moving further away from the crack. Clayton's survival distracts everything around him. He doesn't even seem to notice we're here. Something splashes from inside the crack with a moist sizzle. Bubbling water? No. An orange hot hue of lava blows in the air, barely touching the ceiling above. Most of it falls back into the crack, but puddles of it splatter the concrete into deformed polka dots.

"We need to split," says I. "Barrett and Shawn. You guys help us look for the fire axe. Search the front in the concessions, furnace room, Library of Skates—"

"The what?" Barrett says.

"The skate sharpening room. Me and Ash need to search elsewhere." Before Barrett and Shawn split from me and Ash, I spit one more crucial fact to them. "Whatever you do, don't go inside Locker Room One."

"What's in Locker Room One?" Shawn says.

"You don't want to know."

They slam into the concessions area. Me and Ash chase behind to enter the excruciating long hallway. That's where I meet Danny sprinting towards us under the swinging caged lights.

"Liam?" Danny says.

"Danny," says I. "It woke up."

"Again?"

"We need to stop it. Can you help us look for the fire axe?"

"It's in the zamboni room. I need to get the keys." He runs away. Me and Ash sprint the excruciating long hallway; takes us back to warmups before games, racing down the hall during slouchy stretches.

We tie each other at the game doors. When we smack through the doors, the rubber padding splits in half. The crack from the quake widens into a giant gap, not something we can simply hurdle over. Clear paths to the zamboni room dissipate within seconds. By the time we'd get behind the player's benches, the gap would have crackled it. The only way is to break through the fire exit doors in the long hallway and run around outside.

"Come on," says I. I pull Ash's shoulder to gain his focus back. We pull the game doors open and turn right. The fire exit doors fork to the left at the end. The opportunity slips away like water stealing the puck from our stick's blade. A burnt figure zombie-walks from the forked-off corner. His skin peels in browns, reds, and blacks. Blackholed eyes. Some of the skull shows. It's Coach Kipp. He has the fire axe in his grasps. The bulky blade drags on the floor, but it rises with his ghostly perception. He locks eyes with me. "Go."

We turn and dash down the excruciating long hallway. Coach Kipp chases us down with his axe in his hands. It clicks against the wall as he sways his arms side to side. Our hearts shake with the dangling caged lights as the quake continues to build. The Barn plows us into the wall with a huge rumble. Ash picks me off the ground and pulls me with him. Coach Kipp catches closer and closer to us. We turn the corner to the concessions while Danny runs out.

"Found the keys," Danny says. We shove him into the

Library of Skates. We duck behind the office counter, taking our last gulps of breath before we have to silence into snakes. "What is it?" Me and Ash shush him. No time for an explanation.

"Where's Barrett and Shawn?" says I.

"The furnace room."

The door's shut to the furnace room, but it won't be long till they meet Coach Kipp face to face to zombie face. I peek over the old office counter, and through the musty dust particles floating around, Coach Kipp slows to a walk in front of the concessions.

Shawn's voice flies through the walls and flows under the furnace room's door. Coach Kipp gallops his way to the door and knocks. The door opens.

"It's not here, Liam," Shawn says aloud. The axe penetrates Shawn's head. Blood soaks Barrett as he stumbles, falling to the floor with Shawn. The axe sticks out of his head, and Barrett's eyes stick to it. Ash grabs my arms as I stand, but I rip his grip and sprint in front of the concession stand. Coach Kipp takes his attention off of the axe and looks at me. He starts with a walk and escalates into turbo mode. I fly to the mini hallway and crash into Locker Room One.

The snowbound forest. The cold shivers the timbers. The light casts its white with the overcast clouds. White fluffies fall from the sky like feathers shot from a flying eagle. All peace disrupts when a bloody, disfigured Coach Kipp enters the room. I hide behind the door and watch as a wolf pack sneaks their heads around the trees. My gut tells me to twirl out and lock them in, and so I do. They're sealed inside for a bloody feast. Ash gallops out from the Library of Skates. I run to him.

"Are you okay?" he says. "Is he gone?"

"Yes," says I. "He's gone." Out of the rink's viewing windows, more lava spouts out from the crack in the concrete. "We need to hurry and save Clayton." Danny waits by the Library of Skates, feared like the day I stood up to him and Ben about the steaming blood from outside. His head turns to the sound of whimpers which wisp from the furnace room. Barrett rests his back on the wall, crying in Shawn's blood. I mouth his name as he discovers my eyes. His teeth clatter. I lunge over Shawn's body with the axe in his head and support Barrett. His eyes stay locked on his head as we pass his body.

Ash places a foot on Shawn's head and cracks the axe from his skull. We have the fire axe. "Clayton. Let's go."

We enter the rink and cut through the open section of boards again. Clayton spider-crawls from the spouting lava. Ash stands beside him, raises the axe above his head, and slams on the cords. The air tube above the arena breathes in, blowing up into a bouncy house tunnel. But then, it huffs the air out. The cords tug Clayton's body closer to the lava splats. The tip of his shoe melts as it slides into a puddle. Me, Barrett, and Danny reach for Clayton's hands, pulling him into a tug-of-war. Ash chops and chops and chops, slingshotting the cords to the depths of lava. As a lava sprout sprinkles droplets of lava on Ash's back, he finds an adrenaline kick and throws the axe in fury, chopping the cords like a kitchen chef chopping veggies; *tap tap tap tap tap tap tap*. His mother's body with the disco head shakes into the ravine as she freefalls to

250

the lava pool, deep inside the Earth. Ash strikes the final cord. Tension releases from Clayton. We slide him back from the lava and bring him to his feet.

Before we ditch this place, the divided floor pushes together like puzzle pieces. But the floors aren't shoving into each other, it's being rebuilt. The concrete resolves into a flat surface again. Shards from the disco ball litter the ground, but it's over. We defeated The Barn. But one thing's for certain.

It's not dead.

ROOM 119

Shawn's body disappeared. The Barn ripped him from our hands like Finn and Coach Kipp. Ash understands that the wolf has disappeared too last winter. We don't know where their bodies went. Me, Barrett, Danny, and Ash leave The Barn with traumatized thoughts. This isn't over. The Barn breathes and rests like a human being. It's in a coma like Clayton was in, but only blood and a heart will wake it up again. And it has what it needs. If it wasn't for the burial of Finn's body under the faceoff dot, then none of this would've occurred. But I'm not blaming it on him. There are many I can point fingers at, but what's the use. Someone will end up cutting them off and point them at me.

During the dark night, Clayton reconnects with his father. The four of us leave them to be and roll on over to the best pizzeria in town. Carbone's midnight hour has reached. The place is quite busy while there are midnight specials for beer and appetizers. A waitress carries the menus and places them on our table near the bar. The public ambience of sports shows and cacophonous adults satisfies my comfort. It's been some time since we've lived outside the electric fence. We don't have any more time to spare with our hunger and thirst. Over a day without a real meal and water wears me down. Hockey players need to crave for that balance in their diets. Can't overload on greasy foods before games, but you can't starve yourself either. Bigger snacks or a small meal is the way to go. And water. H2O to go.

When the waitress arrives, we order waters, root beers, and two servings of mozzarella sticks for appetizers. We spill out our three large pizza flavors to her too so they can get cookin. She leaves for our drinks. In the meantime, I feel out of place in the restaurant. No kids feast here. Only adults fill the room while they drink wine, beer, and eat salads and french fries. I'm craving for anything salty. My body can't take the salt anymore, but my taste buds resist anything sweet. A dry desert lives in my mouth.

Tall plastic cups of water sweat on the table as the waitress sets them on coasters. Glass bottles clack on the table as she places the root beers next to our waters. Once she leaves, we chug the water in a heartbeat. Bottoms up, and we replenish. We pop the caps from our root beer bottles and drink with the nearby alcoholics. The bubbles sprout pop rocks into my mouth.

Before Carlie and Casey left The Barn, they told me they would repair the Great Griffin with Steve. By the time the bus gains a new tire, it'll be sunrise. I'm not sure where life will take us and the boys, but we hope to catch up again. Miles and Max will go home with their strict father. Eli and Viktor launch for an elite college this fall. Louie, Thrasher, and Gray will probably prepare for college as well in Minnesota. Eleven may make a journey to the hospital for those chickenpox bites. And Siv, I don't know where goalies go off to. Play for a soccer team? Nah. Teams are desperate for great goaltenders, and seeing Siv play in The Den, he needs to make a collegiate team. He WILL make a collegiate team.

Our two plates of gooey mozzarella sticks arrive. We dig in.

"So, let me get this straight," Danny says. "You guys all went to the same camp with Ben."

"Yes," we confirm.

"And it's not the camp he rejected in the winter, right?"

"I believe so," says I. "Why did he reject that offer?"

"He was scared. He knew the guys playing those leagues were skyscrapers."

"They're monsters," Barrett says. "That's for sure."

These mozzarella sticks explode with flavor. Starving in the wilderness and then coming back home is like moving from the slums to a penthouse in the city.

"What have you and Ben been up to?" says I.

He reflects a *why do you care* face to me, but he opens up. "He gained new friends. I'm not good enough for him anymore."

"Oh. Sorry to hear that." I'm not really sorry. This is what happens in high school with clicky groups. But everyone was stupid enough to follow through with the drama. No one gets in and no one gets out. The absolute worst kind of friendships, especially with a hockey team. That state tournament was never gonna be ours. I bet the trophies didn't even want to frame us.

Pizza finally sits on our table. We dive into the swimming pool of cheese and sauce, devouring the square slices in bites. Weird looks bounce around us, but we continue to feast to the last bite. We debate on dessert, but we decide not to overkill our stomachs.

Danny drives me, Barrett, and Ash to my house in the woods. We sneak to the front door in the cricketing crickets and whooing owls, skimming by without a sound. Mother is definitely knocked out in her room, snoring through the walls. But we too find ourselves snoring through the night with fluffy blankets and plush pillows in the living room.

The wall phone clangs, waking us from our short naps. The sunlight melts a tint of yellow to the morning starry sky. I've woken before my mother. Thought I'd be sleeping in till sunset. I release the blanket from my body, inviting the bitter air conditioning to ice my leg and arm hairs. I grab the phone from its hook and answer. "Hello?"

"Liam," a man says. "It's Steve."

"Oh. Hey, Steve." My eyes grog. I forgot Steve has my mother's phone number. She's a throwback with the home phones. Safe from the scammers I suppose.

"Your friends helped with the flat tire. Your guys are here in front of The Barn, asking for you and your buds."

"Oh, okay. Tell em we're on our way."

For the first time in a long time, I'm back in my SUV. Me, Ash, and Barrett buckle up and head to The Barn. Danny locked it up last night. He was there last night to shoot pucks during the off hours of the arena. But before he locked the doors, he cleaned the remains of the crystals on the concrete and washed the blood from the fire axe. I'm sure he was shivering in the ominous rink, but it looks like he survived.

We park in the lot where the Great Griffin unloads with boys carrying their bags and sticks. Our guys hustle to us. Miles with his jumping cross necklace, and his twinie Max. Siv slow with his bulky pads and bag. Gray with his backwards cap on. Louie strolling his way over to Ash. Eli and Viktor join the group. Eleven and Thrasher are the last ones to dash over. Some of the guys also drop our bags and sticks on the pavement.

Another bruise adds to Eleven's wounds. "Where's Shawn?"

I shake my head and hold his hands into mine. "I'm sorry." Eleven can't discover his tears. I hug him like a grizzly bear. Thrasher closes his eyes and lets the water rain down to the pavement below. Ben exits the bus with Team Ink and groups near the double set of french doors to The Barn. He glances at me, then turns away, avoiding the tears. Avoiding the depression. Avoiding what he wants to avoid.

Days later, Shawn's mother recognizes her son's disappearance. The FBI deployed a manhunt near the forest of Camp Kelmo. They'll find the bodies of two Hunters and a few Team Ink players. They may dig up a younger boy's body. Orson. His parents haven't shown up. Their voices haven't been heard of for a while with the nearby locals.

Barrett's parents are living in a hotel room in Kielstad while they don't have a current home. Me and Barrett ask the register which room belongs to them. Room 119. We drift down the hall, watching the odd numbers on the right wall climb as we make distance. We knock on their door with no response, but the television blares in a high volume. I tell Barrett to stay put as I run to the front desk for a key card. He hands it to me with a little doubt, but this hotel doesn't get too many visitors.

I approach Barrett and smack the card in front of the electronic lock. It beeps on a green light. We open the door to find the news on the television. The sound mixes with a poor reception of static, bashing through our eardrums. We squeeze our hands on our ears and walk inside. Barrett's parents lie on opposite beds with their heads slumped. The air conditioning vent under the window leaks a puddle into a lake. The plastic protector was ripped off from it, and a chef's knife rests on the floor by the sawed-off tubes inside. They poisoned themselves with an AC leak. Suicide.

I give notice to the front desk of the incident. Barrett breaks in my arms. We leave our peace with them. We exit the hotel and drive around Kielstad. We're tired. Exhausted. Drained. Overwhelmed. Nothing seems to matter anymore. This isn't life, but yet it is. Suffering at its finest. Life's a game of war. We learn to fight through it, even through the toughest of times. But the bloodshed needs to come to an end.

It's time to kill The Barn.

END OF BOOK TWO